STONE SCAR

Angeline & Augustine Book #1

T.J. TAO

WordSmith Mojo
Publishing

Published by WordsmithMojo Publishing
Emmett, Idaho

For Angelina, Julia, Tommy, and Tristan... may you never stop dreaming, may you always find life fascinating, and may you always be open to a new perspective.

CHAPTER ONE

August 23, 1805

The numbness in his leaden legs contradicted the nearly unbearable ache that he felt in them. His breath was ragged and impossible to grasp. Will believed he now knew the reason the Shoshone people called this 'The River of No Return', though he would soon find out that he was mistaken. He had no idea... yet. But he did know that it pissed him off to look at Toby, his Shoshone guide, standing atop the peak some fifty feet above him, barely winded.

"You almost here. This last peak before the river enter the stone." Toby cheered him on, in broken but understandable English. He possessed an affable nature that made him difficult not to like. Although he had a few years on Will, he had loads of energy and surprising strength that Will was envious of, at the moment.

Despite the morning chill, Will wiped the sweat from his face and brow. He took one last deep breath before continuing the climb. This 'deer trail' had stopped resembling a trail long ago. It had been two very long days since he and Toby had left the main group at Chief Cameahwait's camp. But at last he was going to have answers to one of the 'special' questions that he had been tasked to explore.

Two and a half years ago, Will's longtime friend, Meriwether Lewis, and personal secretary to President Thomas Jefferson, had conscripted Will to join the expedition to claim, explore and map the far reaches of the newly acquired Louisiana Purchase which ran from New Orleans diagonally to the far northwestern edge of the continent. Lieutenant William Clark, was called in to meet privately with the President. It was that meeting that had led him to the heart-stopping condition in which he found himself.

Will once again launched himself upward, grabbing a handhold as his feet slipped on the loose gravel and rock. The smooth-soled boots on his feet were inadequate for climbing, but two years of marching, riding, and rowing to the west had broken them in as if they were a second skin. Indeed, in more than one spot his feet could be viewed through worn spots on the soles. A native woman who traveled with the group, and who was subsequently determined to be the long-lost sister of Chief Cameahwait, had made Will a pair of moccasins of similar style to those that Toby was wearing. He mentally kicked himself for not bringing Sacajewea's gift with him on this side-journey. He had believed that the hardened leather soles of his boots would fare better against the sharp and slippery rocks that he had spent the last day and a half traversing. Seeing how easily Toby had managed this climb had clarified Clark's foolish thinking, though if he was honest with himself, he knew that shoes weren't the only reason that Toby had made it seem simple.

He reached for the next handhold and struggled to bring his foot to purchase on the hillside. His feet slid and jabbed at the rock looking for a crease or ridge to brace himself upon, but alas with a final slip of rock his feet dangled leaving his entire body-weight on his already bleeding and exhausted fingertips. He began to lose his grip. One finger, then another giving up the fight he was losing the battle. A large, strong hand grabbed onto his wrist. Despite his diminutive stature, Toby was able to pull Will the final few feet onto a small plateau atop the peak.

They were following a spur in the river, an off-shoot cutting sideways into the narrow, rocky canyon's wall. The rapids along the main river had become impassable several miles back. They were forced to follow along the bank, of course in this narrow gorge there really were no banks, only rocks, boulders and mountains. It was said that this spur was 'swallowed by stone', assuming his translations were correct. The tribesmen believed that this river sated the thirst of those in the spirit world, which he took to mean the underworld. Calling it the 'River of No Return' was an intentional effort to keep people away from the area, which also made it exactly the kind of place that he was looking for. The type of place he had been ordered by the President to locate.

Lying flat on his back, finally controlling his breathing, Will felt his body begin to tighten up from all of the exertion. He needed to keep moving lest the cramping and exhaustion debilitate him completely. Toby sat on the edge of the peak completely at ease, gnawing on a chunk of dried meat of some sort, most likely elk.

"Toby, has it always been called, 'The River of No Return'?"

He pointed to the main river, "That one, large water, we call Agaimpaa. To your tongue, it mean 'Big Fish Water'. This water that we follow called

River of No Return. But since no canoe can come down this far, whole thing become known as River of No Return. "

"Has anyone ever come down here, and not returned? Or is it just a name or legend?"

"Yes, many come. None return. After last big snow, three people from our village follow this path. Never see them again."

"Then why are you here, if you believe that?"

Toby shrugged, "I just here to keep you alive."

"Well, I feel like you are failing. Let's keep going. How much further?"

"Not far. Come." he waved Will forward.

Will pulled himself to his feet and shuffled down the narrow path. The water was merely a few feet to his left. The trail was narrow enough that the rock wall to his right scraped his shoulder if he walked straight, so instead he was forced to descend this slope with his body slightly twisted away from the rock face, adding to the discomfort that his body was experiencing. He kept moving. Slow and steady.

A few hundred yards later they came to a large boulder that had deposited itself on the path. Likely quite some time ago if the scattered petroglyphs carved on the surface were any indication. At a glance, the etchings looked like other petroglyphs Will had studied on their journey west. Closer examination, while scraping his nose and face along the rough surface as he reached for handholds to support his tip-toe balancing act as he made his way around the obstruction along the razors edge of the rim of the River of No Return. While his face was pressed against it and he strained to maintain his balance, he noticed some distinctly different marks. Marks that looked suspiciously like runes. He couldn't read them, of course, but he had seen them before at the Newport Tower and several museums. *But that can't be. There is no evidence that Norsemen have been to the west. It cannot...*

That thought was cut short the moment the tiny ridge in the rock that his right hand was using to support his weight detached from the rock, throwing his balance into despair. His arms windmilled as his upper body began to stretch over the gorge as his toes tried to maintain their already tenuous position atop the inch-wide ledge. Will struggled and tipped as gravity took control. His head instinctively turned to look where he was falling, knowing that an unprotected fall like this could be a death sentence out here in the wilderness. Rounded boulders and jagged rocks sat just under the surface of the swiftly moving water. There would be no easy landing here.

A surprisingly strong hand grasped hold of Will's leather vest, stabilizing him, though he was still nearly horizontal to the ledge. He had no leverage, no action that he could take, except to grab Toby around the wrist and hold on. Toby, for his part, held onto a crease in the boulder with one hand, while the other clung desperately to Will's vest. His chest muscles screamed as they contracted, his biceps bulged and seemed to vibrate as he strained to pull the explorer from such an untenable position. Once Will stopped struggling and simply held on to Toby's arm he was able to feel upward motion. Toby let loose a guttural, primal scream as he tugged his new friend back onto the ledge. A moment later, Will was finally able to reach out and grasp a handhold, relieving Toby of the tremendous burden of his bodyweight. He quickly skirted his way around the boulder and back onto the path on the far side. Toby leaned against the rock rubbing his sore chest muscles. Will nodded his thanks, as he was too utterly winded to even attempt to speak. He stood on the path with his hands on his knees as he tried to control his breathing.

"You, Sir, are much stronger than you look. Thank You." wheezed Will. He paced a bit with his arms over his head, still trying to catch his breath. He turned back, "Are you sure you are okay?"

Just then the path crumbled under Will's feet, falling away into the rushing water and taking Will with it.

"William!" Toby shouted after him.

The rapidly flowing water made Will work hard just to keep his head above water, there was no hope of controlling his speed or direction as he was tossed this way and that as if he were a child's toy boat, he crashed into protruding rocks and scraped along the submerged ones. Every impact shook him to his core, only to be immediately whooshed away by the flow. He was a rugged former soldier turned explorer, he was clearly not a fatalistic thinker, but that was changing by the second as he felt his mortality slipping away.

Finally, he gained enough control to point his feet downstream, allowing legs to help him minimize the next impact. He lifted his head to spit out a mouthful of water. That is when he saw it for the first time; a scar burrowed into the stone face of a giant wall leaving an opening the width of the river and nearly level with the surface. A stony beast swallowing the river. He desperately tried to swim toward the right bank hoping to gain purchase and stay out of the maw-like opening.

The river of no return strikes again.

Will took a deep breath of air and felt the current speed up as the river narrowed and sucked him into the hole, his forehead careened off the top of the stone tunnel which caused him to expel the much-needed oxygen that he was holding. The sudden darkness was such that he had difficulty distinguishing whether it was from the blow to his head, lack of oxygen, or merely the state of being tossed through a stone tunnel.

As he traveled through the stone scar, the water spread out into a much wider cavern which slowed the urgent flow of water and allowed him to struggle to the near bank. It took him a moment to realize that he was no longer cloaked in darkness, he didn't notice that the light within the enormous chamber was unlike any lighting that he had ever seen. He noticed neither the change in water temperature, nor the large turbines at the far end of the cavern that the water flowed through to power the cavity within the stone. No, Will was too mesmerized by what those lights revealed; the metallic innards seemed to shimmer as if it breathed. A metal alloy, unlike anything that he had seen in his lifetime of travels, covered the walls and the warm lighting gave it all a golden glow.

No, not covered. The silvery metal is the wall.

The angled alloy walls converged to a point high in the center of the structure. The same alloy seemed to have been used for several pieces of unidentifiable machinery.

Will had dreamt about what this place would turn out to be many times during the nearly two years since President Jefferson asked him to locate it. His dreams didn't breach on the magnificence of what was before his eyes, now. But the ideas and his preconceptions were all wrong, it wasn't what they thought it was at all. It wasn't the boost that Jefferson needed for the struggling economy of his fledgling nation. Despite the shimmer, it wasn't Ciudad de Oro, or Civitas Aurum.

It wasn't the Lost City of Gold at all.

It was infinitely more terrifying.

CHAPTER TWO

May 4th, 2019

He shook his head, as he brushed away the dirt embedded in the scratches. A quick puff of breath cleared out the remaining dust. He mopped the sweat from his brow before shining his flashlight at the marks, moving it around to let the light catch it from different angles. Stuart sighed and turned toward the other two people in the cave, each anxiously awaiting his confirmation.

"No, these are not runes," he reported to his now disappointed colleagues. "Michael, I know you are just eager, but Samantha, I expect more from you. Just because you have unidentifiable marks on a rock doesn't mean they are something special. Most of the time they are nothing. But to leap to the conclusion that you have found runes more than a thousand miles further inland than the closest verified runes, well it's absurd. You have me running out to the middle of nowhere, Idaho, in search of Vikings?"

"But Professor..." Samantha stammered.

"No 'buts', I blame myself. I let myself believe it might be possible for a while."

Dr. Stuart Angeline had been their professor for two senior-level Archaeology courses two years ago at Boise State University. Like many eager grads, Michael and Samantha launched themselves out into the wildlands of their home state full of vigor and hope that they would discover something monumental. Over the last two summers, they had learned that it isn't nearly as easy as it sounds. But they were determined, that much was obvious.

"I don't know how you guys found this cave, but..." he paused and looked around. He wanted to chastise them for wasting his time, but the teacher in him loved their exhuberence and curiosity. "I want you to keep searching... tell me what led you out here in the middle of nowhere, to begin with."

The two youngsters, eager to redeem themselves in the eyes of their mentor, began to speak excitedly over the top of each other and in the echo chamber of the cave it became unintelligible gibberish. Dr. Angeline let them go for a few moments, until one word popped out through the clutter. He stopped them instantly.

"Wait, Cibola? Really?"

"That's what I have been trying to tell you. I know it sounds farfetched, but it is possible. Coronado never found it, not necessarily because it wasn't there, but because he was in the wrong place...maybe." Michael suggested.

Samantha chimed in, "Madison's library is where I came across a reference. James Madison lamented, in a letter to Franklin discussing the dismal state of the treasury, *'If only Thomas' search party had been successful.'* We looked and couldn't find any other 'search party' that Jefferson ever commissioned to the New Mexico Territory, which is where Coronado looked in the 1540s, but he did commission one a bit further North."

"Lewis & Clark did spend time in Kansas and Missouri, where Coronado stalled out, but they spent an inordinate amount of time in Idaho, considering the much larger scope of their public commission. " Michael made quotation marks with his fingers as he said the final words.

Though Stuart Angeline had lived in Idaho for

the last six years, as a biblical scholar, most of his field-work during his career had taken place in the Middle East and Egypt. That is, until he discovered what he believed was the original site of Jerusalem and the real Solomon's Temple somewhere it shouldn't have been. His discovery precipitated an international political incident and a religious crisis, both of which led to a tactical nuke wiping the evidence of the site from the face of the earth.

Certainly, he was aware of the history of both Francisco Vazquez de Coronado's search for the seven cities of gold and Lewis & Clark's mapping of the Louisiana Purchase and the Northwestern Territories, but he had never seen anything that would have, even remotely, linked those two expeditions. His searches, reportedly, had him in what would become New Mexico, Kansas, and Missouri.

"So, what? Do you think Jefferson had some inside knowledge that nobody else has ever leaked? How did any of that lead you here?"

Sam blushed, "I don't have any idea. We simply took our idea and realized that there was no city of gold sitting out in the open, satellites would have seen it, even if people never had. There's a great deal of remote wilderness out here still. We decided to spend the weekends out exploring caves in areas of Idaho that we know Lewis & Clark camped near, in hopes of finding... well, anything, really."

"We've been at this for nearly six months, almost every weekend. This is cave number one hundred eighteen." Michael declared as he held up a spread-sheet which was attached to his clipboard.

"I admire your dedication, but you two should know that while OOP artifacts are found on occasion, it is rare that they were found because someone searched for them. Usually people were searching for something else entirely, and happened upon something that didn't fit."

Out-of-place artifacts (OOPs) are generally things that don't belong in a particular site's place or time. Common OOPs are things like ancient Roman coins in a remote village in Ireland, or a steel arrow-head in a bronze-age dig site. Less common are things like Runes that pre-date the historians' accepted dates of discovery of North America, or Egyptian hieroglyphs in South America, or even Northern Europe. It would be akin to finding a sketch of an AR-15 amongst other primitive cave paintings. Of course, for Stuart Angeline, the ultimate OOP was his discovery of 'Old Jerusalem' some four-hundred miles southeast of where it should have been.

Angeline missed these opportunities to put his Professor hat back on. He hadn't returned to the University after the ordeal in Jerusalem and the aftermath. His visa privileges to Israel and Saudi

Arabia had been revoked, which for a biblical archaeologist was the equivalent of a cyclist that had a leg amputated. Could he do it? Yes. Did he want to spend the next forty years researching from an office, instead of seeing, breathing, and feeling the sites for himself? Hell, no.

As a means of buying his silence, the U.S. State Department had orchestrated a large grant through an off-the-books foundation to fund Stuart's ongoing archaeological endeavors with the caveat that they occurred on the continent of North America. It was a sizable grant, which would be the envy of any archaeological expedition in history, but it also effectively kept him out of the game on an International level. He struggled to find something he was truly passionate enough about to chase.

He excused himself, "Well, I have to go. Keep your passions energized. This wasn't Cibola, but I am certain that if you keep searching you will find something extraordinary. Good luck. Keep me posted."

They all embraced awkwardly and Dr. Angeline exited the cave and embarked on the long hike back to where his vehicle was parked. The walk back brought him back into the very reason he had settled in Idaho in the first place... the natural, largely unspoiled beauty. Despite the spring warmth, the peaks all around him were still heavily cloaked in snow, offsetting the foothills and valleys which were greening up nicely. The wildflowers added a kaleido-scoping palate of colors to the lush green canvas.

Though his native state of North Carolina was strikingly beautiful, most of Idaho was indeed more unblemished by the trappings of man's pursuits. He had been born and raised in and around Raleigh-Durham and created a minor traitorous disturbance amongst his family when he chose UNC-Chapel Hill over his parents' beloved alma-mater, Duke. But Chapel Hill had a distinguished Anthropology pro-gram and access to a number of well-known archeol-ogists who rotated semesters 'in-residence' and 'in-the-field'. This led to a number of internships and opportunities to spend his summers abroad working on actual dig sites. He had no desire to be what he called a 'Museum Archaeologist' working in some office or museum. No, his desire had always been to be in the field, discovering things, as opposed to those who spent their lives studying artifacts that others had discovered. Some of that was necessary, of course, as artifacts found in other places could hold clues to new areas of pursuit, but the focus was on getting his hands dirty and unearthing history.

On the three-hour drive back to his adopted town of Emmett, Angeline could only think of one thing: passion. The passion and persistence that his young former students displayed, in particular. He needed something to be passionate about. The nightmare of short-sighted political and military folks erasing a history-changing discovery had taken the wind from his sails. He had tried to bury his angst through learning about the Native American tribes and folklore, from within his new geographic limits of North American history, over the last couple of years. But he had yet to find something there that grabbed his focus and drove him to anything resembling the passion he had once had for biblical archaeology. He wasn't religious, though he had suffered through Sunday School like every other kid in his neighborhood growing up. No, it wasn't religious zeal. It also wasn't a drive to debunk religion. No his drive was taking a set of stories from two-thousand to five-thousand years ago and exploring how much of it was accurate and how much was corrupted by either the oral traditions of storytelling at the time, or corrupted intentionally by the powerbrokers who drove the expansion and domination of the early Christian and Jewish faiths.

During graduate school he had, of course, studied more broadly; Hindu folklore, Celtic history, Norse mythology, and European history, so there were a number of other avenues that he could have pursued. But in the funk that he was in, he tried to focus on local history and had to admit he hadn't accomplished much of anything in the last eighteen months or so.

He needed something to capture his imagination and reignite his passion. And he needed it soon.

CHAPTER THREE

May 6th, 2019

James panted as his exhalations fogged the rimless lenses of his glasses in the cool early morning mountain air. His exhalations were coming far too frequently and his sides hurt from the exertion. Perhaps he had tackled this particular trail a bit too early in his effort to get back into shape. He struggled up the short steep sections, only to slip and slide down the other side with only the slightest illusion of control.

Two days short of the six-month anniversary of the day that the BonnFire engulfed his hometown of Genna, and really the first day that felt like winter had lost its grasp on the land, he'd decided he needed to get out of the funk that he was in, starting with a nice long hike out in God's Country. He now thought he may have overshot with his first foray into real physical exertion in half a year.

Though he had been hailed as a hero after saving several stranded high school kids during the evacuation of Genna, he never felt heroic. He had tried to stay positive and lift people up, but in the days and weeks that followed it had become clear that living a life that alternated between couch-surfing and living in his car was not a sustainable condition for either his physical health, or his mental health.

He relocated to a small farming community, just over the ridge from Boise, about three months ago. While Emmett was a nice little town, and was beautiful in its own way, it wasn't the paradise he had found in Genna. Though, his time in Genna had given him both a taste of Heaven and a taste of Hell.

He hadn't yet developed any real sense of 'community' in Emmett, which was what he missed the most about Genna. Instead of jumping in and getting actively involved in his new community, he chose to isolate and hide from the feelings of loss. He had met a few of his neighbors, and they were nice enough, but he hadn't really connected with any of them. He did everything exactly the opposite of how he had been taught in his years as a member of

Alcoholics Anonymous. Everything except drink, that is.

He struggled through his period of darkness, but was now making a conscious effort to rejoin the world. The first step in that journey was to go where he felt more of a spiritual connection than anywhere else, out in nature. Now, his next step was not to drop dead of a heart attack while he was hiking toward his own personal spiritual vortex.

James crawled up a shale-littered embankment and when he reached the peak, he promptly sat down on the edge and let his legs hang off the side. Though winded and tired, it felt great to get his blood pumping and now, to sit here looking over this little valley. To commune with nature, and the God of his understanding. Though it was a small peak, it was tall enough to see glimpses of the Salmon River winding its way through the rocky hills about a half a mile to his northeast. He could see snow-capped mountains in every direction and long-dormant trees in the valley were just beginning to bud. Spring had arrived, and with it a renewed urgency for James to figure out what to do with his life. He had mourned the loss of everything he knew for long enough.

James grabbed the tube that hung across his shoulder and pulled it into his mouth for a long pull of water from the camelback backpack that he wore. He grabbed a protein bar from the side pocket of his pack and took a bite as he sat and enjoyed the peace and stillness. A slight breeze blew bringing a chill to his sweat covered body, but it was a refreshing chill. Invigorating.

He closed his eyes and just listened for a few moments, before uttering a short prayer of gratitude. He was grateful. Grateful that nearly everyone that he knew survived the fire, against overwhelming odds. He was grateful that he had made it through his funk over the winter and was still sober. Grateful that he had his mantra:

Only by Losing Everything, Do I gain the Freedom to Build a Life of Uncluttered Purpose.

Those words had appeared to him sixteen days after the fire, as he looked upon the ashes of his home for the first time, and he knew that they were words to live by. What he didn't know yet, was what his purpose was. Once he found that out, these words would be his life rules. You don't often get the opportunity to start your life over from scratch.

James was shaken out of his reverie by the majestic sight of a bald eagle swooping down to snag a rabbit scurrying down a path towards a hole in between some rocks. It bounded valiantly and bounced from rock to rock before dropping into the hole just as the eagle's talons were snapping closed a hair's breadth away from its neck. The eagle, unflustered by his miss, continued on its graceful arc back up into the cloud spotted sky and out of sight.

James, however, refocused his attention on the path that the rabbit had run on. He mentally kicked himself that he had missed a way around this peak which, had he known it was there, would have made his hike much more pleasant and much less taxing. Then again, he would have missed the view from where he sat. It was worth the climb, but he resolved to find the path on the way back. *No point in suffering needlessly.*

He pulled his smartphone from the pocket of his cargo shorts and snapped a few pictures, knowing that the pictures would never do justice to the beauty that he saw before him. He stood, stretching his aching back as he did so, and brushed the sandy gravel from the back of his shorts and legs. He glanced at the path ahead. Only one small ridge and then a decline down into the valley below. He took another small sip of water and continued on his trek.

Born James Aloysious Augustine to English and Irish parents who were huge fans, and distant relatives, of Irish writer James Augustine Aloysious Joyce, he had been a good athlete in his younger years. But now, at the age of fifty and coming off of a five-month run of being an uncharacteristically professional couch potato, he was feeling the side effects of that sedentary lifestyle. As he reached the bottom of the last slope his legs felt like rubber.

James could see small herd of elk grazing near the tree line, the largest one turned to keep a close watch on what James was doing. James shook his legs out briefly and turned right, in search of the rabbit's trail. Within a few hundred feet he reached the pile of rocks that the rabbit had disappeared into. The formation of hundreds of rocks of a multitude of sizes were precariously balanced at random angles. The rabbit's natural safe-haven appeared to James to be the result of an ancient landslide, a few hearty plants had grown and fully developed in the dirt-filled spaces between some of the rocks.

He continued wandering down the path, absentmindedly noting the trail of rocks and boulders that formed their own path from the rabbit pile down the center of the valley, alongside the path. Or perhaps, it was the path that ran along the side of the rock river. The other side of the path was worn into the rockface that he had perched himself atop earlier. James glanced at his watch; he'd been out here for nearly three hours. He needed to get going if he was going to get home before dark.

James continued down the path, around a bend

and came to an obstruction. A rock slide covered the path. As James looked for a way around that didn't include climbing down into the rock gully, he noticed something strange. It made him stop and run back to the large rock pile that was the rabbit's lair. *Nope, totally random.*

He sprinted back to the trail's slide and knelt down beside it. The rocks on the bottom were lined up, as if placed there deliberately. They weren't randomly strewn like the other pile, but built like a foundation. The top layer all appeared random, but the bottom layers were much too perfect. *Definitely man-made. But why?*

He took out his phone and snapped a few pictures of the oddity, then continued on his way.

CHAPTER FOUR

August 23, 1805

Will struggled to keep himself from being drawn back into the flow of the river. He couldn't quite pull himself up to look over the ledge, yet he had the sense that there was nobody there. At least, not in the immediate vicinity. The eerie golden glow gave the place an otherworldly vibe and the sound of the rushing water almost drowned out the sound of some kind of machinery whirring...almost.

The surreal nature of what he could see made him briefly wonder if he was dead or unconscious and his mind was merely conjuring up such a vision, but the bone-shaking chill of the water told him that this was not the case. The lighting was bright enough that he could see the far end of the cavern; he could see how the river narrowed before shooting into another tunnel, which he presumed led outward.

He needed to get out of the water before hypothermia set in, but he could only see three options, none of which seemed to have any assurance of his survival.

The easy route would be to simply let go, and see where the river took him. Uncertainty initially made him lean toward ruling that option out, then he remembered what the Indians called this place, *The River of No Return*. No, that option didn't give him the warm fuzzies, at all.

The second choice would be to try to climb out into whatever this facility was and see if there was another way out. Of course, he had no idea if there were unfriendlies here that might react to his intrusion in a place that was clearly meant to stay secluded from the world. He was also weaponless, save for the sheathed hunting knife attached to his belt. Not to mention the fact that if he did somehow get out, and avoid encountering any hostiles and another exit wasn't found, he would be forced into choosing one of the other two exit options anyway.

Climbing back out the way he had come, against the water-flow would be the most physically taxing, but offered a set of known variables that the other options did not. He knew that it led out, he had survived coming in, and Toby would likely be there to help him on the other side. Of course, he was already struggling to hold onto the rock wall with his cold, weakening fingers, and that was without the force of the narrow water chute that he would have to work against. He seriously doubted he could manage it, but William Clark was no quitter. He had been in impossible situations before, and had always managed to keep his cool.

Perhaps, I can climb out and just rest for a few minutes before I jump back in and attempt it.

Suddenly a fourth option appeared to him. The end of a rope snaked through the center of the river, bobbing up and down in the current, trolling like a fishing line flowing downstream. Clearly, Toby hadn't given up on Will just yet. The rope was well beyond his reach, at least fifteen feet away, he would have to swim for it. The current moved swiftly out there, the question was, once he left the relative safety of his rock wall, how far downstream would he drift before he reached the rope? Once he was there, there would only be one chance to grab it, if he missed, he would be washed through the length of the cavern and out the other side.

Will worked his way upstream, along the ledge until he was well above the end of the rope. He found a solid handhold and twisted his body so he faced out toward the center of the river and pulled his knees up with his boot soles planted firmly against the rock wall. He took a deep breath to ready himself for the perilous swim, calmed his mind, and exhaled slowly. He gathered himself and started an internal countdown, 4...3...2...

On two, his grip slipped and though he instinctively kicked off the wall with his feet, his launch was significantly stifled by the slip. Will dug in and put his head down as he swam with everything that he had. Kicking his water filled boots, wearing his heavy long-drenched clothes, and suffering from mild hypothermia his mind slipped from feeling confident that he could make it, to panic as he realized that he wasn't going to make it to the center before being swept past the rope. William Clark was no quitter. He jabbed his hands out in front of him into the water, one after the other pulling his body through the water with each stroke. He could swim faster with his head down, unfortunately with his head down he couldn't see the rope. As the water tugged him downstream, Will put his head down for three more strong strokes before lifting up and seeing the rope end just a yard or so in front of him, he needed one more big pull or all would be lost. The current had swung his legs around below him, downstream; he lowered his head to make a final push directly into the oncoming torrent. One big pull and he slapped his hand into the water where the rope should have been, but it came away empty. He had lost his battle.

He started to make one more stroke, but as he pulled his arm back into his body, he felt something foreign slide across his forearm. Will frantically spun his arm around in a circle and wrapped the rope around his wrist before deftly, and desperately clamping his hand on it. His body jerked as his downstream momentum stopped. He swung his left arm up and grabbed onto the rope with it as well. As he did so the rushing water shifted, due to the 'obstacle' that he had become, rush up his arms and over his head as if he was a rock beneath the roaring rapids. He found it to be a great deal of work simply to get his head into position to take a breath.

He felt the water speed up momentarily before realizing that it wasn't the water changing speed. He was moving. Moving in jerks and lunges, but moving nonetheless. The tugging of the rope tightened it around his wrist. He stopped struggling and straightened his body out in line with the rope then he kicked his feet vigorously in an attempt to aid whoever was pulling the other end of the rope, presumably Toby.

Inch by agonizing inch, Will kicked and moved out of the main cavern and into the darkness of the stone tunnel. He rarely had the opportunity to take a decent breath inside the tunnel, but was able to find occasional footholds to propel himself forward. He kicked, and pushed, and held on to his lifeline until finally he broke through into the light of day. Sputtering and gasping, he finally took a deep breath and saw Toby, still straining with the rope wrapped around a boulder and his own waist, leaning back before lurching forward to grab the next section of rope and using the leverage of his weight and the boulder to lean back again.

Will immediately worked his way over toward the side of the river gorge. Eventually, he was able to climb out and up the rocks before collapsing on the path. As for Toby, he may not have been winded climbing the hills earlier, but he certainly looked beat now. Still, he had his ever-present smile as he looked at his shivering friend splayed out in the dirt.

"You the biggest fish Toby ever catch." He jeered.

"And you, my friend, are my savior once again. Maybe I need to take you on the rest of the expedition with me." Will laughed.

Toby shook his head vigorously, "No, keep you alive is too much work."

They both laughed.

The two men, now bonded for a lifetime, took a

few minutes to catch their breath then ventured back up the trail, toward their camp site.

Toby's curiosity broke the silence, "What you see in there?"

Will, pondered this question. He didn't want to lie to the man that had just saved his life, twice. But this part of the mission was classified, only Will and Meriwether Lewis knew of President Jefferson's interest in this location. The truth was, that Will wasn't sure how to describe what he had seen even if he had wanted to. It was unlike anything else on this planet, or so he thought. In the end, he decided to bridge the gap between truth and omission.

"I can't really even describe it. It was... it was surreal. A long dark tunnel, lots of rock and water. From what I have seen, I am not surprised that nobody has ever returned from in there."

They trudged over the two ridges back to camp mostly in silence, in part out of reverence for the experiences that they had just shared, but also because Will racked his brain trying to explain what he had seen. *Light within the cavern, but steady light without the flickering of torches or candles. And what kind of metal gleams like that? More importantly, who built it, and what was it?*

As they crested the last hill, Will could see one of the two braves, that they had left behind to watch the camp and care for the horses, using a handheld net trying to catch fish. The second brave was slumbering leaned up against the base of a tree.

Will, not wanting to risk any miscommunication with the braves, turned to Toby, "Can you send one of them back to Chief Cameahwait's camp and have him bring Meriwether and a courier here? Make sure that they understand the urgency. Leave the rest of the expedition there, just bring Meri, and a courier."

"Yes, I understand."

While Toby dealt with the runner, Will dug his leather-bound journal out of his saddlebag intent on documenting his find. With his pencil clenched between his teeth, he flipped to the next blank page, grabbed his pencil and... nothing.

He had no idea how to describe what he had seen. He also wasn't sure he should.

CHAPTER FIVE

May 6ᵗʰ, 2019

James, pulled into his driveway, narrowly dodging the brown garbage canister that the sanitation guys had left in the way. It was a nicer two-story home in one of the only subdivision neighborhoods in the rural farming community of Emmett.

It was an ideal neighborhood, in every way: friendly people, well-kept properties, and quiet. Still, for James Augustine, it didn't feel like home. The last six-months had felt like he had been floating through the motions of life waiting for something. Anything, that would help him move past the horrors of what had happened in Genna. Alas, while the Feds were cleaning up most of the debris and ash from the devastated town, thousands were still living in trailers, tents, and cars. Indeed, James was one of the lucky ones, though he didn't often feel that way. His heart was still in the paradise that had been Genna.

His legs were stiff as he unfolded them from his car, and then took the trash bin around to the side yard. The neighbor next door was mowing his lawn and waved as James dragged the can behind the gate. Suddenly the mower went silent.

"Hey James, I was about to throw a couple of steaks on the grill. You're welcome to join me. It'll be sort of a belated 'Welcome to the neighborhood' meal. What do you say?"

"That sounds great! I just got back from a long hike, let me grab a quick shower and I'll be over in a bit. Can I bring anything?"

"Just whatever you're drinking. I have everything else covered."

James showered quickly and began scouring his kitchen for something to take. Before he had gotten sober, there was always plenty of wine in the house. Easy pickings for an impromptu dinner gift, but his life wasn't that simple anymore. He opened the fridge and sighed: half a bottle of Diet Coke, three hard boiled eggs and six one-liter bottles of sparkling water. He had had more food than this when he was a starving college student. He opted for two orange flavored sparkling water bottles.

Feeling somewhat guilty, he departed for next door.

After a couple of fabulous ribeyes, the two near-strangers discovered that they had quite a bit in common and chatted amiably. James wandered to the bookcases; envy threatened to turn into victimization at the thought of losing his book collection in the fire. Most of the books were old history and reference books, in fact there were no new books on the entire case, most were well-worn leather-bound tomes. There were various artifacts on display as well; old urns and pottery, the occasional silver pendant.

"So, what do you do for a living?" James inquired.

"I'm a biblical archaeologist... or at least I was. I suppose I am just an archaeologist now."

"Very cool. I have always been a history geek myself. Have you been to any cool digs?"

Stuart measured his response, "You wouldn't believe me if I told you."

"So, what changed?"

"Suffice it to say that throughout history religious academia has often been stifled by the political powers that be. Apparently, that hasn't changed in the last few thousand years. They don't like discoveries that might upset the apple cart. And I tried to flip the apple cart over on its head."

"What did you find?"

"I can't say, it's been classified Top-Secret. They even made me sign a non-disclosure agreement. At any rate, it has been wiped off the face of the Earth, anyway." Stuart's eyes drifted off into the distance, lost in thought.

James could see he had touched on a sensitive subject and decided not to spoil the mood by pressing further.

"What are you working on now?"

"Nothing specific at the moment, some dig consulting. I have been focused on learning more about the indigenous tribes here in this part of the country, their customs and folklore. Honestly, I have been kind of spinning my wheels."

James knew all about spinning his wheels and the inability to commit to a plan of action. He had done a great deal of that since the fire. Just then, he remembered what he had found on his hike.

"Hey, I know this will be boring to someone like you. But I found something interesting on my hike today. I can't quite figure it out. Will you take a look?" He fished his cell out of his pocket and thumbed his way to the appropriate picture.

"I was hiking up near the North Fork of the Salmon River and there was a rock slide covering part of the trail. No big deal. But as I was trying to work my way around it, I noticed that on the bottom, all of the rocks were much more ordered, like they were placed there intentionally. See."

He handed the phone to Stuart, who he knew was only humoring him. Stuart looked and immediately saw the anomaly that James had described.

"Yes, I see what you mean. I suppose it could have been some sort of alter or monument before the rock slide. That would explain the highly organized foundation stones. Or it could have been some sort of burial marker. It's hard to say."

Stuart, his duty done, started to hand the phone back to his new friend but stopped short when something caught his eye. He pulled the phone back and spread his fingers on the screen to zoom in. He unconsciously sat forward in his chair as he scanned the image. *It can't be.*

"Tell me this isn't a prank."

"What do you mean?"

"You found this just today?"

"Yes, why?"

"This morning I went up north to see something that a couple of my former students thought they had found. They thought they had discovered runes in a cave. I quickly dismissed it and chastised them a bit for being overzealous. You see nobody has ever found runes or runestones this far inland, or this far west for that matter. The Kensington Runestone would be the closest at around eleven hundred miles, and that's if you believe that it is authentic. Many don't."

"Okay, what does that have to do with my rockslide?"

Stuart smiled, feeling the excitement of his chosen field for the first time in what felt like ages. He spun the phone around so James could see the zoomed in phone.

"See those marks there peeking through between the rocks? Those, my friend, are runes. I would bet my career on it."

James had, of course, heard of runes though he didn't know much about them. He knew they were a form of language for Druids and Vikings and probably some other peoples, and he had seen the Newport Tower in Rhode Island when he had visited several years ago. There had been an exhibit about Runes, and while he found it interesting at the time, apparently, he hadn't found them interesting enough to remember any of the details.

"So, what are they doing out here in the middle of Idaho?"

"I have no idea. But I hope you aren't busy tomorrow."

"Not really. Why?"

"Let's go on an adventure and see it for ourselves."

CHAPTER SIX

August 24, 1805

Despite his exhausting day, William Clark had hardly slept a wink last night. His thoughts and visions centered upon the golden glowing room within the mountain. *What could it be? How did it get there?*

Oblivious to the early morning chill in the air, Will was antsy. He paced from the campsite to the river and back several times as he awaited word that Meriwether was nearly here. He had sent Toby up to the nearby pass early in the morning to watch for Lewis. *He should have been here by now!*

Will finally sat down and leaned against a large boulder. Still bursting with restless energy, he unsheathed his knife and pulled out his sharpening stone and strap. Once he got into a rhythm the long slow strokes as he slid the steel edge at an angle along the coarse stone calmed him somewhat, or at least gave him something to focus on. It was almost a form of meditation.

A few minutes later the sound of galloping hooves pulled him from his single-minded concentration.

"The Captain comes. Soon he be here, Mister Will."

"Thank you, Toby."

Shortly the clip-clop announced their arrival. One of the Indians tended to Meriwether's steed while the other three managed their own horses.

"William, please tell me that you found it!" Captain Lewis boomed.

Will looked around nervously, unhappy with Meri's indiscretion over a classified discussion. Meriwether picked up on his disapproval and followed up, only slightly more quietly, "The savages don't understand us anyway. Come on tell me."

Will looked apologetically in Toby's direction. Toby rolled his eyes and shook his head ever so slightly with his typical good nature, despite the insult. Will didn't respond until Meri had reached him, and Will led him away from the group toward the river.

"I found what we have been looking for, but it isn't what he thinks it is."

"My goodness, it really does exist then. Magnificent!"

"Well, yes... and no."

"Well, lad, which is it? Is it here, or isn't it?"

Will bristled at being called 'lad'. He was four years older than Captain Lewis, being called lad felt like Lewis was talking down to the lowly Lieutenant. He knew it wasn't meant that way, but unlike during their time in military service, Lewis was the appointed Commander of this expedition.

"The golden city is, indeed, here." He paused trying to find the right words, "but that is not the same as being a City of Gold."

"Well, what is it?"

"Honestly, I have no idea. I don't even know how to describe it. I thought all night about how to tell you, and the President about it. I can't find the words. The only way, is to show you. And I think I figured out a way. But I am going to have to bring Toby into our confidence on this."

"Why Toby?"

"Because he saved my life yesterday, twice. And we may very well require that again today. But also, because I think Toby knows more about this place than he lets on."

Meriwether nodded, "Let's go see Cibola!"

They helped Toby gather all of the rope that they had, and the three of them began the hike along the *River of No Return*. Once again, Toby led the way, showing no sign of the extra burden of the equipment that he carried. Lewis followed eagerly while Will struggled from the fatigue of the previous day's exertions and the sleepless night. On the way they filled Toby in on this piece of the mission. He took it all in quite nonchalantly.

In due time, they made their way to the path, stopping only to show Meriwether the various carvings in the boulder on the path. Though Lewis wasn't an expert, he was well-read and had received enough education that he knew that all the markings on the stone shouldn't be all in one place. The styles and glyphs were from distant lands and he couldn't fathom a reason that they could possibly all be here in the middle of an unexplored part of the North American continent.

Once they reached the stone scar, where the river flowed into the rock Will announced, "Well, here we are."

"What, here?"

"Well, technically... in there." Will replied and pointed at the maw. "How did you describe it yesterday, Toby? Where the rock swallows the river?"

"You go back in there again; you find spirit world for sure." Toby opined.

"Maybe, but that is why you are here, my friend. To pull us back from the brink." Will winked at him.

"So how do we get in?" asked Lewis, though he suspected that he knew the answer.

"Meri, you're a man of science. We will be utilizing a combination of velocity, surface tension and gravity."

"So, we're riding the river?"

"You got it. We are riding the river."

The trio got to work laying out the various ropes that they had brought, along the length of the path. They knew that the rope Toby had utilized the previous day was long enough, but the others were much shorter. Even joining the other three didn't give them quite as much length as the other one.

"It will have to do. Let's tie them off to that boulder, Toby can't handle both of us. Meri, you tie the long one around your waist. I will take the shorter one and loop it around my wrist."

"Will, let's just wait and get more rope."

"I have been in there. I know what to expect. You need to see this. We have decisions to make."

Will confirmed that the ropes were secure, then helped Meriwether wade into the rushing water. "Get your feet pointed downstream as soon as the current sweeps you off. And breathe until you enter the tunnel then hold your breath as long as possible.

You'll know when you get where you need to be. It's a whole new world."

The cold crept up their legs and Meriwether's teeth began to chatter, though he wasn't certain if it was a result of the cold, or nerves, excitement, or outright fear. He accepted that the likely answer was all three. Following Will's instruction, he sat back into the current and let the river take him. *Cibola, at last!*

CHAPTER SEVEN

May 7ᵗʰ, 2019

Trudging along the path that James had found the day before, the two spoke little. James noticed Stuart had a bit more pep in his step than he had the night before. James had to admit there was a strange excitement of anticipation that he felt at the thought that his accidental discovery might, in fact, be something historic.

"We're almost there. It's just around this bend."

Dr. Angeline already had his analytical mind humming. He studied the dry riverbed alongside the path. He knew that was what it was due to the erosion of the rocks and the way that they were dispersed along the same stretch of land. Rainy season erosion of the cliffs on either side of it had deposited a fair amount of sediment in the gorge; essentially cementing the rocks together and making the riverbed smooth enough to be its own path, with the exception of some wild grasses and a few sparse bushes. Clearly, it had not been a running river branch in quite some time.

Shortly, they came around the bend and reached the blockage on the path. Dr. Angeline whipped out the camera that he brought along to document the find, an older Nikon D-3100. It was a solid camera, but technology advances in cameras for smart phones had long rendered it obsolete. Still he preferred to have the ability to choose from multiple lenses, stored in his shoulder bag, to allow him to get the best shots possible in various conditions. He snapped a few general photos of the rock slide from the side. He wanted to shoot it from every possible angle before they touched anything. The edge of the path had worn away and he was forced to balance on some stones down in the gorge to get a picture of the outward facing side, before climbing back out to capture the far side.

James joined him beyond the blockage. "See..." he pointed to the base, "these are the stones that drew my attention."

"I do. And look in this hole." He pointed to the

space between several stones. "That is the Rune that I saw on your picture."

James could clearly see etched into the stone a straight vertical line with a downward diagonal flag coming off the top. It looked to him like the right half of an arrowhead. It also didn't seem all that out of place since this had long been Indian territory. Drawings of arrows should be commonplace.

"An arrow head?"

"Well, yes. Kind of. It looks like *laguz*, one of the Elder Futhark runes. It means water, or lake. Although until we see if there are more, I can't say for sure. It is a simple symbol and I would imagine that multiple cultures used it for something. We need to see if there is any context, or other markings. Let me get a few more pics, then we'll figure out how to unstack some of these rocks without the whole thing coming down on us."

Uncertain of the stability of the rock pile, the two opted for a top-down approach. James deftly climbed up the pile until he was able to balance precariously atop it. Rocks wobbled under his feet causing him to kneel down on all fours. He started by rolling one off the side that faced the riverbed. It crashed and bounced down the slope, taking two more stones with it, before coming to rest in the gorge. Feeling a bit more confident, he shoved another off the same side. It too loosened a couple of additional rocks, all of which landed safely in the riverbed. Emboldened further, James swung his feet around in front of him and, with knees bent, dug his heels into two of the gaps between several rocks. He assured that he was well balanced and sitting firmly, then in a quick motion straightened his legs as if he were at the gym doing leg presses. Two, three, five rocks went over the side at once. Unfortunately for James, as those stone bounded down the side and picked up additional stones, one of those must have been the keystone that held the pile in place.

"Look out!" he shouted.

Dr. Angeline leapt backwards, landing on his backside, as the entire pile seemed to release all at once, pouring down the three sides away from the cliff face as they thumped, scattered and rolled into the gorge and onto the pathway alike. The noise, like a freight-train on a wooden bridge, shook the ground as the gravity driven avalanche came to a halt and inertia once again reigned. A cloud of dust enveloped them causing Angeline to sputter and cough for a moment.

When the dust cleared, he looked up to find James sprawled out on his belly across the top of a massive black boulder, whilst his legs dangled off the side.

"Well, that was not exactly what I planned," James laughed sheepishly.

Dr. Angeline, didn't hear him. He was instantly mesmerized by what he saw. The beauty, the grandeur and the utter impossibility of that he was looking at shook him to the core.

"Get down from there. Very Carefully." Stuart called, his voice distant and detached.

He began clearing stones from the path at the base of the boulder, so that he could examine the rock more carefully... and so James had a place to land. Once James slid off of the rock, he dusted himself off then turned to see what had captured the Professor's attention.

An oval-shaped chunk of black obsidian stood on end, rising some ten feet above the path. Aside from the dust that had collected in the grooves, it gleamed and shined in the noon day sun, as if it hadn't spent centuries buried under several tons of dirt and rock debris. The sides had been completely smoothed as if it had been placed on a massive lathe. There were things carved into the smooth surface that seemed fantastical. He put a finger out to touch one, to reassure himself that this was real. James had no idea what any of it meant, but he thought it was cool to find something so unique out here in the middle of nowhere.

Dr. Angeline, on the other hand, was muttering to himself incoherently, as if he was in shock and unable to formulate actual words. James picked up a few, "Unbelievable, but … it can't…magnificent."

Finally, the mumbling stopped. Stuart looked at James again, as if he didn't trust him. "And you really just found this yesterday?"

"Hell, I didn't even find this. I found a weird pile of rocks. You found the carvings."

Stuart's skepticism was flashing red lights in his mind to alert him of one of those finds, those career killers, that are simply too good to be true. Of course, his discovery of *Old Jerusalem* had been too good to be true, as well. But despite the destructive aftermath, it was real. He had walked in Solomon's temple and placed his hands on the great bronze columns, Boaz and Jachin. He knew in his heart, though his brain had not quite accepted it yet, that this was legitimate. Whatever its origins, or meaning, or purpose what he was looking at was truly, for him, a second chance.

"This is impossibly remarkable." He exclaimed finally.

"Yeah, it's pretty cool. I have never seen anything like it."

"Nobody has. There is nothing, that has yet been discovered, like this in the entire world. Look at these markings."

James was looking, but he had no idea what he was looking at. "I hate to say it but it looks a lot like the carvings that bored teenagers make on picnic tables. Of course, this isn't wood. What makes it all that unique?"

"The runes up here, " he pointed before continuing, " those alone would make this a magnificent find. But look, there are Runes, Latin inscriptions, pictograms, hieroglyphs, Roman letters, Greek letters, Sanskrit, and several symbols and languages that I can't identify without reference. I suspect one or two of those symbols will turn out to be of Hindu origin."

"Cool."

"Not just cool. It's not about any of the individual inscriptions or etchings. What makes this so utterly unique is that languages from different eras and from all around world are all represented here in one place, out in Middle-of-Nowhere, Idaho. It's as if this was some historic waypoint or crossroads and this was the guest log. If this was in Istanbul, or Jerusalem it might make sense. But here... it just doesn't fit." He tailed off, lost in thought.

"I guess you should take some more pictures and we can find somebody to translate them, see if the meanings tell us anything about its purpose."

That pulled the Professor out of his trance-like state, "Yes, yes. We'll need lots of pictures."

Angeline went to work, like a fashion photographer trying to capture the money shot. He shot from different angles and with different lenses, zoomed in close, zoomed out, individual images, the works. In five minutes, he was certain that he had gotten enough shots to document a complete record of the find.

The day was beginning to get short, although this time of year the sky tended to stay bright until after nine o'clock at night. Still, they had a long drive ahead of them to get home. But Stuart had no desire to let this surreal experience end. This was the beginning of whatever he was searching for that would reignite that fire in his soul. He just knew that this was it.

It suddenly occurred to him that this isolated stone couldn't be the only thing in the area. There had to be some purpose in its existence.

"James, did anything else catch your eye out here?"

In his mind's eye, James pictured the majestic bald eagle swooping down after the rabbit. He was certain that Stuart wasn't interested in bird-watching. "Not really. I was sitting up there." He pointed to the peak above the path. "That's when I noticed this path down here. An eagle was dive-bombing after a rabbit. The rabbit ran down the path and jumped into the rabbit hole around the bend, in the other rock slide."

"Like this?"

"It's bigger, and more random. None of the foundation stones like this one had. It's right over here, I'll show you."

The two hustled around the bend and a few hundred yards. The hillside before them was taller than the others along the river, with a sheared-off face that culminated in a large pile of rock at the base covering both the path and the river bed. The slide was a magnitude larger than the slide that had covered the inscribed boulder.

Stuart walked around the base of the slide looking for any indication that this was something more than what it appeared to be. There was nothing to be found. Gingerly, he climbed up the rock slide to get another perspective. Again, everything he saw told him it was a natural rock slide. He stood at the very peak, atop a large triangular stone and looked down upon the gorge. James was down near the rabbit hole trying to lure the critter out with a long weed and strange squeaking noises.

"James, there's nothing here. We should probably get loaded up and head back."

He began to step down from the triangular stone, suddenly it wobbled causing him to lose his balance. He stepped over to the next stone with one foot, to find some stability. As he did, the triangular stone slid just a bit and knocked into the stone next to it. Suddenly, both stones dropped into a hollow space. Stuart leapt onto the next stone barely maintaining his balance as more stones collapsed into the growing hole. He moved delicately to a third stone searching for stability.

"Stuart! Look out!" came a frantic shout from below. Stuart didn't need the warning; he could see it coming. The rest of the peak collapsed in on itself pulling the Professor with it.

Stuart felt the thud as he hit the bottom, flat on his back. He looked up at the pinprick of the new skylight as it faded instantaneously as it swirled into an inky darkness.

CHAPTER EIGHT

August 24, 1805

Meriwether sailed on the strong current of the frigid river, bounding over the occasional bump of a shallow rock. He saw the opening of the stone scar approaching more quickly than he expected as his journey accelerated. He gripped the rope even more tightly as he took the last moist, deep breath and rushed into the unknown and the darkness.

Will rushed into the maw of the cavern moments behind, and narrowly missed cracking his head on the entrance again. He held his breath and the rope, and said a quick prayer. After just a few feet absolute darkness swept over him.

His lungs screamed for him to breath, but Meriwether held out until he was suddenly thrust into the golden glow of the facility's lighting and a moment later jerked to an indelicate halt as the rope went taunt. The violence of the stop involuntarily expelled the air that he had been holding, but the water rushing over his head made it difficult to draw the next breath without coughing and choking on it. He dangled on the end of the line, and began to panic as he was unable to move himself out of the current and over to the calmer edges of the underground river.

Will Clark, too, held his breath. He could just see the glowing light ahead, at the end of the tunnel, when his momentum came to an abrupt stop which caused the rope to slip from his fingers. He had come up short, and raced untethered into the cavern. He struggled to control his movement and he slammed into Meriwether. The collision bounced the two of them apart and Will continued unabated downstream. Franticly, his hands scrambled for something to slow him down, his left hand caught onto Meri's boot at the last instant. He spun over and grabbed onto it with the other hand as well.

He lifted his head up to get his bearings, as the water continued to rush over them. He could see his partner's hands working in a frenzy trying to untie the knot, without success. The extra drag of

Will hanging off his foot had pulled Meriwether just inches deeper, but those inches put his face under the water. His friend was drowning, in front of him.

Will shifted position and kicked with all his might as he tried to maneuver them both out of the main current, into the calmer waters near the edge. Once he had better stability, Will went to work on Meriwether's knot. The water-soaked rope, under extreme tension, didn't want to release. He knew that they were in trouble; Meri was in trouble. Having had no luck on the knot, Will whipped out the knife from his belt and crawled up Lewis' now-limp body and with one strong swipe across the taunt line, severed the rope and breaking them both free. He had to tread water as he moved his Captain toward the edge.

Suddenly, Meriwether coughed and sputtered as his lungs cleared and he drew in fresh oxygen. His eyes popped open and he began to struggle.

"I've got you Meri." Will said as he tried to calm him. He swam them toward a boulder which protruded slightly from the water. He hoped with all his heart that they would be able to make the leap from the boulder to the raised platform which formed the floor of the cavern.

"Oh my..." Meriwether gasped as he took in the glowing metal structure for the first time. "What kind of metal is that? And where is the light coming from?"

"Pull yourself onto that boulder, then you can gawk all you want," Will panted. Between his water-logged leather trousers and water-filled boots, he was beginning to struggle to keep himself above the waterline, much less trying to carry the Captain, too.

Meriwether pulled himself up onto the flattened top of the boulder. He stood and took his first real look at the facility. The cavern seemed to extend farther than the few machines that they could see, but there was no telling how far it went. Nor did he have any idea what the purpose of this place was. It was otherworldly.

"I can see why it's called the City of Gold, that amber light gleams off of it. Or does it come from within the metal itself?" He gazed around in awe. "It's unbelievable, utterly remarkable. But I don't think it will solve Thomas' funding problems, as he had hoped. I also don't see anyone here, so why is everything lit up?"

"We should proceed with caution and assume that we are not alone," Will whispered. "I have a bad feeling about this place."

"It's not like we are armed, anyway. If there are people here, then we are at their mercy. We must hope that they are men of honor."

"I'm not even convinced that they are human. This place is far beyond us. We should probably just find a way to shut this place down and move on."

Will climbed up onto the boulder alongside Meriwether. He wasn't sightseeing, he'd been there and done that. He wanted to go explore. That is, after all, what they were commissioned to do. The jump from their perch onto the landing was dangerously far. He scanned the area and noticed something that he hadn't before. There was a flat landing immediately adjacent to where they had entered the cavern. They had overshot and it had gone unseen. The water between the two was calm and protected by the stones, a private pond of sorts. He leapt into the relatively shallow pool and waded toward the landing.

"Come along, Meri. I found a way up."

When he reached the platform, he crawled up it and saw that there was a short set of stairs, carved into the bedrock, that led up to the upper platform. He marched up the stairs as Meriwether was struggling to pull himself onto the platform. In a moment, he was walking across the platform to go look at the machinery, eager to determine what they did. All of the equipment seemed to be made of the same magical metal used in the main structure was constructed of. One piece of equipment was humming slightly; a reminder that they may not be alone.

"What in God's name is this place? Meriwether asked rhetorically. He walked right up to one of the beams and reached his hand out to touch it. The metal pulsed slightly, and while it appeared as strong as steel, it also seemed to move with his touch. The light emanating from it changed briefly where his hand was. "Who could have created this?"

Will didn't respond, he had wandered over by the equipment. He didn't understand any of it. There were no moving parts that he could see. There were flat panels with strange symbols moving across them. "How do these signs and things move? They seem to be made of light, but they keep changing their position. What are they for?"

He wandered over to the next 'thing' beyond the glowing screens. A ramp ran up between two tall gleaming posts, all of it was made of the same strange metal as everything else. But the air between the posts seemed to be disturbed. It wavered ever so slightly and distorted even the nothingness of the dark cavern behind it. He could feel a kind of energy coming off of the contraption, though he would be hard-pressed to describe what he felt.

"Meri, what do you think this is for? The air around it has ripples, like the river. Like when it gets very hot outside and you see the sun bend."

"This entire place is either madness, or magic. It is certainly unholy. But to what end?"

"Yes, indeed. To what end?" Will echoed.

The two stood side-by-side as they walked up the ramp, as they reached the pinnacle there was a brief flash... then they were gone.

CHAPTER NINE

May 7th, 2019

The rabbit darted out of the hole, once again missing his demise, as the pile shifted and collapsed.

"Professor!" James shouted, as he watched his friend and the top of the rock pile collapse out of sight. He received no response.

James waited a moment until the rock pile stabilized again, then gingerly climbed up, carefully trying not to disturb anymore stones and send them down onto his friend. When his head came even with the gaping hole he gazed down into the gloomy abyss. He couldn't see anything. He heard nothing. He decided that the only way for him to get to Stuart, without falling in himself, was to start widening the hole. Carefully, he grabbed a small stone from the rim and pulled it backwards, letting it roll safely down the pile. He peeked back over the edge to ensure that he hadn't let anymore fall in as he did so. He saw two glowing eyes staring up at him from the murky darkness.

"Professor?" he queried. He heard a groan. "Are you okay?"

After a moment of silence, a restrained voice replied, "I'd say the term, okay, is relative. But I am alive."

Everything hurt. Stuart was trying to take a physical inventory to see what the damage was, but every part of his body ached. He wiggled his fingers than his toes. He tested his ankles and wrists, then his knees and elbows. Everything ached, but everything seemed to work. No significant pain, simply the kind of pain that a forty-five-year-old should feel after dropping fifteen or twenty feet and landing flat on his back.

"Can you move?"

"I'm working on it." Came a reply with more edge to it than he had intended. He carefully rolled onto his side and pulled himself up into a sitting position. "Well, I'm going to be awfully sore for a few days, but it looks like nothing is broken."

"What can you see down there?"

James watched as Stuart powered up his cell phone and turned on the small flashlight function. "Not much, it just looks like a stone tunnel."

"Can you back into it? I think I can bring this pile down, but I want you to be safe."

"Yes, just make sure that you don't come down with it. There will be nobody left to rescue us."

Stuart shuffled back into the tunnel and sat down on a boulder. James examined the rim of the opening. The ring now was quite solid with the rocks tightly packed together, but he knew that one of them would be the kingpin that held the whole thing together. Now he just had to figure out which one, and not die when it all came tumbling down. He chose one in the middle, at least from his perspective, then perched his bodyweight and center of gravity further down the pile and tried to work it out. No matter what he did, it wouldn't budge. He decided on another stone. It too stubbornly refused to move. He shifted his weight back up and tried to get better leverage on a third rock. With next to no effort the stone tumbled into the pit, after a momentary delay another fell. Suddenly the entire pile imploded and collapsed into the tunnel entrance like pouring out a bag of marbles, rolling down and spreading out. James rode down with it, in a terrifying drop down the chute he slammed to the ground. Luckily, because of where his body had been positioned, he stayed above the falling rocks and rode down atop the stones.

Bruised and battered, James came to a rest only a few feet from Stuart's feet. "Well, that was less graceful than I had hoped."

"Well, from here it looked easier than trying to dig out one rock at a time." Stuart teased.

"I bet it did. I hope you're comfortable. Can we get out of here now?"

Stuart pointed at the rock pile that had covered the opening. James turned to look and saw that the tall pile had been transformed. The entire shape of it had transformed. The center of the pile had collapsed with James, leaving a large 'V' shaped opening in the center, whilst the edges were still standing tall. They would be able to simply walk out through the doorway.

"Great let's get out of here."

"Yeah, I need to grab my pack. I have a couple of flashlights we can use."

"It's still light enough to walk back to the car, without a flashlight. We'll be ok. Let's go." James offered.

"The flashlights aren't to get to the car."

"What do you mean?"

"I have been thinking. On your hike, did you see any other rockslides on the area?"

"These two are more than I have seen anywhere else."

"That's my point. Though it does occasionally happen, this area isn't really prone to rock slides. But to have two in the same vicinity; one that just happens to cover a really unusually carved boulder, which itself doesn't seem to be like any of the other rocks around here, and a second which happens to cover the opening to a stone tunnel. This doesn't seem to be coincidental. Somebody blocked this tunnel and intentionally hid that boulder. That, in my mind, intimately connects the two."

James didn't necessarily like what he was hearing.

"We need to see what is in this tunnel that they tried to hide. Let's go back to the rock and get our packs."

They went back to the engraved boulder and retrieved their packs. James dug a couple of bottles of water out of his, one of which he handed to his new friend. After taking a swig, he glanced around and made another connection.

"This stream or river or whatever it used to be would have flowed right into the mouth of that tunnel. Maybe the State was just redirecting the water to keep it flowing down the Salmon River. This could have been an Army Corps of Engineers project."

"That's possible, but if they dammed it up at the

river, why go to the trouble of covering the tunnel? And that doesn't explain the inscriptions. I am hoping that something in that tunnel will definitively connect the two."

Despite his fall, Stuart seemed to be re-energized. James, was ready to be done. It was fun playing the 'discoverer' of the cool boulder, but it had already been a long day. He was beat. He had been hopeful that he could get back into town in time for his evening AA meeting. That didn't look likely. He closed his eyes for a moment, not necessarily to pray but to quiet his mind and listen. He had learned to truly believe that things always worked out exactly how they were supposed to, whether he liked them or not. If he was here and about to embark on this exploration, then there must be a reason for it. He had a purpose for being here, the fact that his higher-power, which he chose to call God, hadn't shared exactly what that purpose was didn't surprise him. He rarely knew the 'why' of anything until he reflected on it. It became clear in his mind that he was exactly where he was supposed to be. That was enough.

He shoved the water bottle back in his pack, and with his attitude and mindset readjusted he said, "Cool, let's go check it out."

Stuart, on the other hand knew, in his gut that this was something that he needed to do. He had been searching for something to bring the passion back to his work. He had floundered around for long enough; it had been a couple of years since the Jerusalem fiasco had stolen his passion. This was the kind of mystery that he had been searching for ever since. He had no idea where this would lead, or even if he would find anything in the tunnel but he knew that the inscripted boulder would provide months of work for him to translate, decipher and decode. It was fascinating that so many cultures could be represented on something sitting out here in the middle of nowhere.

The two walked around the bend and back toward the tunnel. They entered through the wedge-shaped opening and clicked on their lights. Once they cleared the rocks that had dropped into the opening, they swept their beams back and forth along the walls of the tunnel. It was surprisingly even and smooth.

"This is strange. It's like the tunnel bored out of the stone. It appears perfectly round and smooth on the top half. But the bottom half, where you can see where the waterline was, it looks more natural, eroded, but not perfectly cylindrical like the top portion."

Though James thought he was talking to him, he noticed Stuart was speaking into a handheld digital recorder, documenting what he saw. James had noticed the walls being smooth but had missed the difference between the two halves. He focused on being a better observer and to take in the details. Maybe he could be of some help.

They passed a boulder with a flat top as they entered into a larger chamber. James' flashlight was pointed up, but didn't reach the top of it. Stuart continued straight down the riverbed until they reached the end of the cavern, documenting what he saw every step of the way. He stopped short. "James, look at this."

He flashed his beam ahead of him, a glare flashed back at them. Four strangely finned machines shined, as clean and dustless as if they had been newly installed. They looked like turbines of some sort.

"How is it possible that these aren't coated in dust? Clearly, they haven't been used in some time. Was this an old power plant? I have never heard of one being built into a mountain; they are used in dams."

James wasn't listening. From his position his flashlight found more gleaming equipment up on a ledge. "I don't think it's a power plant. At least not one of ours."

Stuart wheeled around, "What do you mean, 'not one of ours'?"

Then he saw where James was pointing his light

and added his flashlight to the mix. Up on a ledge above the waterline stood several pieces of machinery, all seemingly just as shiny and clean as the turbines. He moved his beam around and noticed the metal lined walls and beams that were embedded in the bedrock which culminated in a tall peak.

"They've built a pyramid? Inside this mountain?"

"A better question is: who is 'they'?" James replied.

James shined his flashlight over to the left side of the ledge and noticed the stairway. "Let's go up and check it out."

They made their way back across the cavern, around the flat-topped boulder, and up the stairs. As they rose, it became apparent that, despite the new looking metal, nobody had been there in ages. Their boots left distinct foot prints in the thick dust on the stairs and across floor of the upper chamber. They were able to get a better view of the metallic structure from the platform as well, shining their lights up at the pinnacle where the metallic beams all converged and joined. The Professor finally made the connection.

"This is a pyramid, of sorts. How and why would anyone build a pyramid inside a mountain?" He gasped, sounding awestruck.

James placed his hand on one of the vertical support beams, "It's kind of like stainless steel, but clearly it is some other alloy." Suddenly he felt is vibrate slightly under his touch. He swung his light onto his hand and could see the metal moving and bending under his hand. He removed it and the metal bounced right back into its form. "It's almost like a solid liquid. Which makes no sense, but it is moldable or something. I don't know how to describe it. Did you see that?"

Stuart nodded, suddenly unsure of what this place was. He kept moving forward across the cavern toward the machinery. They, too, were made of the same strange metal. They too were completely dust-free despite the buildup on the floor around it. Not a single spiderweb or cobweb adorned anything in the facility, again muddying the ability to gauge either the age of it, or how long it has been shut down.

Suddenly, they heard a scuffling sound in the riverbed and they realized hadn't heard anything the entire time they had been in the cavern, except themselves. They both spun around at the noise, which sounded especially loud as it echoed through the place. Their lights swept around the riverbed, seeking out the unseen visitor. James' light came to a stop at the entrance to the tunnel, where the small grey rabbit, who lived between the rocks, sat watching them intently.

"Hey, little guy. Are we intruding in your home?"

Stuart move back to checking out the machines. There were a couple of vertical glass plates seemingly hovering above what he assumed were controls for whatever this machine did. In his mind it was the control panel and a monitor, but in reality, he had no idea. All of this was a guess at this point. Everything about the place looked both old and modern, futuristic even. His mind couldn't conjure up an explanation as to which was correct. Could something be both old and this advanced? He had a brief thought about the show, *Ancient Aliens*, but dismissed it immediately. *Follow the facts, Stuart. Follow the facts.*

James had wandered over to the next machine. Atop it was a single piece of paper with a handwritten note, dated more than two hundred years earlier held in place by a fist-sized semi-opaque stone.

CHAPTER TEN

August 24th, 1805

Lewis & Clark were suddenly facing down the ramp and heading down into the chamber.

"Did you feel that?" Will asked.

"It was a flash and a wind gust, then we were suddenly turned around. But there is no wind in here. That was strange."

"It's about to get stranger."

"What do you mean?"

"Silence."

Meriwether listened; the silence was deafening. They had gotten so use to the sound of rushing water that they had tuned it out. Its absence was terrifying.

"Where did the river go?"

Will, ever nonchalant, remarked dryly, "The question, is where did we go?"

They had entered another chamber, nearly identical to the one they had been in. Nearly.

The machinery looked virtually the same, though placed at slightly different angles. The metal structure glowed the same golden glow and a slight hum echoed through the area. But it was definitely not the same place they had just left.

"Perhaps, this was just another chamber that we didn't see."

"It is definitely another chamber, but let's find a way outside and see if we can figure out where we are."

The two walked to the edge of the platform and down the stairs. To their right was a seam in the stone of the mountain. They wound their way through the maze of a tunnel and soon could see light emanating from an opening ahead. Will tensed, unsure what they would face when they exited the tunnel. Meriwether was still in denial, this had to be part of the same mountain. It just had to.

When they reached the opening, Will put his hand up signaling for them to stop. He put his finger on his lips and whispered, "Stay put, let me go take a look."

Will exited and stepped out into the sunlight and the humidity struck him immediately. When his eyes adjusted to the brightness, they opened wide.

"Meri, come out. You've got to see this!"

Lewis appeared alongside him and looked out at the... well, he didn't really know what it was.

On the hillside below them, an old village sprawled out, just above the trappings of a rainforest whose canopy spread as far as the eye could see. The villagers were dressed in tribal duds, not totally un-like those of the Indians the two had gotten to know so well. Though their skin and hair were dark as night. Grass roofs topped some of the small structures. Others had large, elongated leaves woven together that served as rooftops. There was a large central cooking pit in the center of the village, with smoke rising above the rooftops.

They could see birds soaring above the canopy, colors standing out against the deep green backdrop like drops of paint on a canvas. The sun was just be-ginning to set, out on the horizon. It was stunning from their vantage point.

"Should we go introduce ourselves?"

"Are they friendly?"

Will looked askance at Lewis, "How should I know? But we either go introduce ourselves, or we go back into the cave and try to figure out how to get back to 'our' river of no return. Which do you prefer, Captain?"

"Oh, stop with the, Captain, nonsense. You know Thomas will set things straight when we get back."

Meriwether was right. Calling him Captain had become something of a jab for Will. Thomas Jefferson had indeed offered Will, a Lieutenant, a promotion to Captain and the status of co-commander for this expedition before they left. However, the Army had reneged on the promotion so as not to cloudy the chain of command. Clark was a bit bitter about the whole ordeal. Though the jabs were seemingly thrown at Lewis, Will knew that his friend had nothing to do with the decision. In fact, he had vehemently voiced his opinion that the Army review the decision. But at the time of their departure, they had not reported any change of heart.

"Sorry."

"I know. Shall we go down?"

The question was answered by a blow dart swooshing through the air and embedding itself into the mountain only inches from Meriwether's face. Several more thunked all around them as demons leaped from the ledge above them down onto the path, blow guns and spears at the ready.

Will was an accomplished fighter, and Lewis was

more capable than he appeared, but they found themselves overwhelmingly outnumbered, as each time they heard another muffled sound of bare feet making an impact with the ground.

These demons looked nothing like the Indian warriors that they had seen. They seemed even more primitive and primal. Faces were painted a ghoulish white, with red and black streaks going diagonally across. They wore skirts of animal skin and had necklaces with animal teeth dangling from thin leather strips. One, had a necklace which had intermittent shriveled ears hanging on it. Several had sharp pointed claws where fingernails should have been. Savagery shone from their eyes. They grunted, clicked, and squealed in a syncopated manner.

For their part, Will and Captain Lewis tried to look non-threatening and non-aggressive with their hands above their heads, in what they hoped was a universal sign of submission. Meriwether was fairly adept at tribal languages, but even he couldn't make head nor tail of what they were saying. One thing, however, was obvious. They weren't happy to see them.

They were forcibly restrained and marched down toward the village. Will tried to get a feel for the strange men. They were all lean and most were well-muscled. None of them even really looked at their captives, they faced forward in something akin to a trance.

As they entered the village, the villagers scattered grabbing up the children and disappearing into their huts. Their faces showed a deep seeded fear, but Will couldn't determine if they were fearful of them, or their captors. The normal village folk weren't painted up, nor did they seem aggressive like the warriors that surrounded Will and Meriwether. And with such an entourage, why would they be fearful of two simple strangers. He suspected that these guardians, or warriors didn't venture into camp often.

They were led to an open, but roofed, structure near the central cooking pit. The smell wafting over the area was unusual, yet not necessarily unappetizing. The two were pulled to a stop and the men fanned out around them with their weapons ready. At the far edge of the gazebo-like structure was a stand with an enormous, curved hollowed out tusk of some sort, adorned with multi-colored painted designs and decorative opaque stones. One of the warriors, the most muscular one who seemed to be the leader, put his lips on the tip and blew four mighty notes through the horn. Then stood at attention and waited, fear shone even in his eyes. Seeing that fear in the leader stirred the first bit of fear in Will, until now he had simply been biding his

time until the inevitable interrogation and negotia-
tion that he had experienced dozens of times with
the Indian tribes he had encountered. He suddenly
got the impression that they were dealing with
something very different here.

"I have a bad feeling about this." He whispered
to Meri, "No sudden movements, but follow my
lead." Meriwether simply nodded in response; his
eyes riveted to the edge of the rainforest where the
warriors were all staring... wondering what it was
that they had called.

After several minutes of standing, unmoving as if
they were statues, all of the men knelt simultaneously, save for Will and Meriwether. Still, Will saw
nothing moving that could have triggered the genu-
flection of the warriors. For a moment, he considered making a run for it though he knew it would
likely make the entire encounter more painful in
the end.

A high-pitched flute-like whistle sounded as two
people, not as dark as the natives but with similar
facial features, appeared dressed in flowing robes
and spread apart some large leaves that had blocked
a pathway from view with large staves.

Cloaked in deep red and gold a lone figure
emerged from the path, his sandaled feet walking
upon flower petals lain by three scantily-clad women
that looked to be in their mid-teens − one pale, one

dark skinned, and one that had the same coloring as most of the Indians that Will had seen. The primped man, tall and clean-cut, appeared to be in his thirties called out to the leader of the warriors, in his own tongue, "What have you brought for me, Tmboku?"

"White men come through demon gates." He replied in confident clicks and grunts.

The man switched to heavily accented English, "Well, they don't look like demons to me." He looked directly at the two captives, "They think you are demons. Are ye demons?" he asked with a smirk in his voice.

"Not last I checked, but I suppose it depends upon one's perspective." Will retorted.

"Touche`."

He clicked and grunted several times and all of the warriors, except for Tmboku, the leader and two others who stood shoulder to shoulder with the prisoners, scrambled back up to their perch up above the cavern's opening.

"Why did you come here?" He got direct and suddenly less witty.

Will and Meriwether shared a glance. "To be honest, we don't know for sure how we got here. We don't even know for sure where 'here' is. I'm Lieutenant William Clark and this is Captain Meriwether Lewis. Who might you be?"

"Do you really expect me to believe that you haven't come here to try to stop me?"

"Sir, with all due respect, I have no idea who you are. Why would I be here to stop you?"

The man laughed, "Let me get this straight, you accidentally stumbled on one of the most complex and advanced machines in all the world and somehow you got it adjusted properly and ended up here... in my kingdom." He waved his arms in an expansive motion that somehow clearly indicated everything that they could see was his.

"Partially, except we didn't adjust anything. We simply walked up the ramp and we were here." Meriwether chimed in. "Where exactly are we?"

"Ah, introductions are in order. I am Andres David," he stretched the last name out as 'Dahveed', "God-King of the Kingdom of Hasabi."

"Blasphemy!" Meriwether muttered under his breath.

Andres's harsh stare rebuked Lewis' insolence. "Perhaps, but gods are created by man and these men have revered me as a god, their God, ever since the day I stepped through that portal some one hundred and thirty years ago."

"Wait, one hundred thirty years?" Will interjected. "That can't be possible."

"More is possible in the world than you can possibly imagine."

King Andres seemed to weary of the conversation, "You two will dine with me tonight at the palace. Then we will decide your fate." He glanced over toward the cooking pit. "Unless you would prefer to dine with the Hasabi."

The two captives followed his eyes with theirs, which instantly opened wide when they saw a blackened and charred human body on the grates of the cooking pit. Will's stomach turned at the sight, and the 'not unpleasant' smell became very unpleasant, indeed.

Their host turned on his heel and as the three girls laid a fresh path of flower petals, he returned to the path from whence he came. The two were relieved of their knives and lashed to separate posts within the gazebo with woven-vines and each was left with one guard standing directly next to them as Tmboku grunted and stormed away.

Thankfully, the sun was setting and the oppressive heat began to recede, though the evening brought with it its own issues. The air was thick with flies and mosquitoes, and aggressive ones at that. With bound hands unable to swat them away, they simply had to endure the onslaught. The humidity soaked their shirts in sweat. The guards seemed immune to the aerial attack and stood unflinching in their duties.

After about an hour, though it felt much longer

to the two captives, the foliage was parted again and the pale woman and the one with Indian coloring emerged from the path, each carrying torches and a pail. After handing the torches to the guards, the two each knelt next to one of the men and with some sort of sponge began to clean their faces and neck in an almost ritualistic fashion. The water had a slight fragrance to it: citrus and fresh flowers. It was somewhat refreshing and instantly the flies and mosquitoes ceased their hitherto relentless attack. Though it made Will briefly wonder if they were cleaning them before dinner, or basting them for dinner.

Meriwether spoke to the pale one as she scrubbed his forehead. "Thank you, do you speak English, young lady?"

She momentarily looked him in the eye, as if understanding, then broke the connection and continued washing his face.

"How long have you been here?"

A sudden forlorn look of sadness appeared in her eyes, but quickly she shook it off and stood. She grabbed the torch from the nearest guard and said something brief. The guard pulled what looked suspiciously like a Sioux tomahawk from his side, Meriwether had been gifted one nearly identical to it just a few months ago, and swung it with expert precision to split the vines holding him to the post.

Will was similarly released and the two were pulled up to their feet. The women waved for them to follow as they turned back toward the path in the jungle. The guards followed until they reached the path and then abruptly stopped and stood at attention as the four wound their way into the torchlit jungle. There were torches placed on either side of the path at intervals, though Will couldn't determine if they were there to light their path, or to keep the jungle predators away. Though he had never seen one, he had heard stories of the monstrous cats and creatures that called the jungle home.

"How do we get out of this?" The Captain whispered to Will.

"I don't know, yet. But I want some answers from this god-king before we go."

The Indian-looking girl turned and put a finger to her lips, silently urging them to keep quiet. They trudged the rest of the way in silence.

Soon they saw a glow amidst the darkening jungle and as they reached a clearing, they saw the palace, a strange balance of primitive and opulent. Torches surrounded the property as did a new set of guards, dressed in flowing robes of orange and purple.

"They must be his personal guard." Will muttered.

The palace itself was constructed of stone primarily, but it also had a large wraparound porch and elaborate carvings and sculptures lined the walkway and up the stairway to the entrance. Though vines grew over the roof, it was apparent that the roof was covered with clay tiles. The light shone from within even more brightly than it did out on the grounds. They were led up the steps and through the doorway. They entered into a large entryway. Meriwether nearly jumped out of his skin when he saw a large white tiger pacing along one side of the room, a chain fastened him to the wall, but still it was shocking to see. A candlelit-chandelier hung at the center of the high ceiling. Just inside the entrance the two girls stopped. The pale-skinned one walked over to an identically designed, but smaller version of the tusk-horn that had been blown at the gazebo, and blew three notes into it, announcing their arrival.

A double-door at the end of the foyer opened wide. "You may enter!" a voice boomed and echoed off the stone.

They followed the two women through the doorway. The women stopped and genuflected before retiring to either side of the doorway. Lewis & Clark kept walking. Will was use to negotiating with Indian chiefs and was use to following their traditions and showing them the same respect that their followers gave them, but he had no intention of bowing before this man who claimed to be a god.

It was a spacious room with a long dining table in the center made of well-oiled wood. Several chairs ran along each side culminating at a large golden throne at the head of the table. Two place settings were set on either side, at the far end away from the throne where a third setting was placed. Their host stood just behind the throne chair in an even more elaborately decorated robe.

"Ah, my guests have arrived. Welcome to Castello David. Please have a seat." Andres motioned to the two settings.

Will glanced at the paintings on the walls. Paintings that looked familiar even to his uneducated mind. They were copies of famous paintings, but the face of Andres David had been painted onto the heroic scenes. It was a sure sign of narcissistic hubris, but they did make an impression. A Persian rug covered the majority of the floor adding to the confusing impression of primitivity and grandeur.

"It appears we are underdressed for such an occasion," Will quipped. "Perhaps we should return home and don proper attire."

"We shall have to make do with you as you are." Andres stated as he moved himself around and into his throne. Will and Meriwether took their places.

Immediately, a native man came out to pour wine into the goblets at the table.

"Judging from your accents, I can see you are not English. So, you must be colonials, yes?"

Meriwether answered first, "Not anymore. We kicked ol' King George's troops back across the sea. Our country is now known as the United States of America."

"King George, eh? Hmmm, time has a way of getting away from me here, Charles II was king when I first crossed over. How in the world did a handful of colonials with pitchforks throw off the reign of the British? Fascinating."

"When you say 'crossed over' what exactly do you mean? Where are we? And how can you have been here that long when you look no older than we do?"

"It feels like an alternate universe, but really it is simply a different place. Here we are in the center of the African continent. Just a few steps up the ramp and you traveled half way around the globe. Or through it to be more precise. If that is possible, then nearly anything is possible, wouldn't you agree?"

"I believe that nearly every question has a practical answer. How are you not aging?"

Andres reacted angrily, "Because I am a GOD!" he yelled. Just as quickly he got control of his emotions and resumed his confident cool demeanor. "Look around you, who but a god could civilize these people and put them to work in such a remote place? Who else could bring them modern and antiquity together in such a way? Who else could bring such riches to these savages?"

The King gripped the arms of his throne. Will noticed that they flexed and bent as he did so, yet bounced back into shape as soon as he let go. It wasn't gold at all, it was the same metal as they had seen in the cavern.

"How did you acquire all of these accoutrements? I assume that you came through the portal with only what you had at the time, like we did. And that throne, how did you learn to work with such a strange metal?"

"Quite so. But one-hundred-thirty-years gives you a great deal of time to tinker and figure out how to work the thing. I have made trips back to various places over the years. Ironically, while these diamonds have no value here, I have amassed quite a fortune in the outside world."

"Diamonds?" Will asked.

"Look around you. The rough opaque stones that decorate everything are uncut diamonds. The natives mine them for me. They offer them to me as tribute to their God."

Meriwether suddenly spoke up, connecting a few

dots in the narcissistic raving of the madman, "Wait, you said 'to various places', there are more... what did you call them, portals? More than just Cibola and this place, whatever you call it?"

King Andres suddenly looked like he had said too much, but quickly covered himself. Cibola? Are they still calling it that in your time? Ha, 'cities of gold'." He smirked, "Mankind's biggest limitation is that his greed directs him to the wrong treasures. They set the bar so low with gold as the world's primary addiction."

Several servants appeared bearing trays of food for each of them, and stopped to serve the God-King first. Lewis & Clark shared a glance when they received theirs. The meaty bone that sat centered amongst fire roasted vegetable of some sort brought back visions of the charbroiled human down in the village, which nauseated them both.

Andres must have picked up on the sudden change in their demeanor, and savored their fear for a moment, then erased their concerns. "The human was for the Hasabi, not for me and my guests. I assure you that a wild boar's ham hock is quite tasty. Do eat up, while you can?"

The two, still cautious, braved the first bite. Then seemed to gain confidence and devoured the meal with little small talk. At the end of the feast, Will broke the silence, "The Indians of our land call the tributary that feeds the portal on our side, *The River of No Return*. I take it that we aren't the only ones to have crossed over?"

"No, no, we do get visitors from time to time. Most are savages terrified of their own reflection. Most end up being served to the villagers and warriors. Some, however, are worthy of conversation first, and a few others have been kept for breeding."

The fact that he could speak so brazenly and unremorsefully about feeding people to his cannibalistic subjects reminded the two captives of exactly the type of man that they were dealing with: sadistic, cruel and unflinching, despite the moments of charming joviality.

"These young ladies, are they all your daughters?"

"Come now, all of the people in the realm are my children. The children of God. Isn't that what the Christians and Catholics teach you all still, or has religion somehow shifted since my last confession?"

"While I will admit it has been quite some time since I have been in a proper church, I believe that this language is still used, yes." Meriwether said tensely.

"Well, then. There's your answer. You two are the first visitors that don't look discombobulated at being thrust into this new world."

Will chimed in, sensing that the meal was

coming to a close. "Well, Sir, with all due respect. We have been through a great deal over the last decade or two, very little surprises or phases us. Though we have never dined with a god-king before, so I appreciate the opportunity to do so. If I may be so bold as to ask, will you allow us to return to our own land and complete our expedition to the Pacific coast? We will leave you in peace, you have our word."

Andres looked amused at the question, as if his wicked mind was busy conjuring up a scheme for them. "Again, you mortals ask the wrong questions. You should be asking whether you will live out the week. You certainly won't be going back. You will never go back. I will ponder whether I have a use for you here. Though I suspect that you are too dangerous to keep around. My guards are bred for not only extreme physicality, but extreme brutality, and loyalty is ingrained in them from birth. I don't see you fitting in well with them. But I will grant you free roam of the village until I have made my decision, but do not test me. Do not venture off the path or the jungle with take care of you even faster than my guards would. Enjoy your evening, it may be your last." With that parting shot, King Andres stood from his throne and departed through the far doorway, a guard immediately shifted position and took his place in front of it.

Bewildered by the turn of events, the two captives stood shaking their heads. Will held a finger to his lips, making it clear that they would talk later, not here in this place. Meriwether was clearly flustered so Will leaned in close to whisper, "Don't fret my friend, I have a plan to get us out of here and deal with the so-called god-king all at once. It's a pretty good plan... maybe."

"Pretty good?" He questioned forlornly. "Well, that's better than anything that I have come up with, I suppose."

CHAPTER ELEVEN

May 7th, 2019

James read the hastily written note from the browning, brittle paper.

August 27th, 1805 Warning

For the safety of our flejling nation and for civilization at larg, we have disabled this facility and hidden its location forever. Obviously, if you are reeding this note, forever was not nearly long enuff. The river opens the doorway to gods and deamons, alike. Be warry and walk away.

Sincerely,
Lt. William Clark

"Professor, look at this."

Stuart came up beside him and took the piece of paper. "Is this 'THE' William Clark?" James asked.

Angeline read the note through once, and then again, whilst unconsciously holding his breath. "I would have to double check, but the date appears to be about right for when Lewis & Clark were in this area. And I would say that the language he used looks authentic. I know someone who can verify it. Despite his many successes, Lt. Clark was always embarrassed about his lack of formal education, and being that most of what we know about him came from his writings, well, let's just say that whatever sounded good to him at the time was how he spelled it. I remember reading somewhere that in his journals about the expedition he spelled the word 'Sioux' something like twenty-seven different ways."

James stepped over a pile of what appeared to be construction scrap: rocks and metal and assorted material, as he walked over toward the two poles which flanked a ramp that peaked about four feet above the ground surface. He walked up to see what was on the other side. There was nothing there, but floor that stretched back to the chamber wall.

"How do you think they hollowed out this

mountain? It was solid stone, I think. But this is almost too perfect."

"I thought it might be an old volcano, but I don't see any evidence of that. It's definitely, strange. I have no idea."

The Professor flashed his light around the cavern and finally sighed. "Now that we know what we are dealing with, kind of... we should probably get out of here and get back to home. I want to gather some halogen lights and some other tools and come back so that we can actually see what we are looking at. Plus, I want to send pictures of the Waypoint Stone to a friend at Boise State, a linguistics expert, and see if he can come up with anything. In Downtown Boise, there is a Lewis & Clark Museum and we can at least verify the signature and handwriting on that note. Then we can come back up properly prepared to investigate. Are you up for it?"

"This is kind of a big deal then?" James replied.

"It could be, I really think it is. Unless this was a government shutdown, then they may very well shut us down again. But I think this has amazing potential. The fact that we have no idea what we even found makes it even more fun. Plus, with my foundational grant, I can bring you officially on-board as a partner on this, and even pay you. What do you say?"

"Sounds like an adventure! An Angeline & Augustine Adventure!" James quipped.

They grabbed their packs and started walking back toward the stone tunnel.

Later that evening, James was just coming down from the excitement of the day when he received a text from Stuart.

I just printed out the pictures, holy cow, there are something like thirty languages on this stone. Even Aramaic, which is my specialty. Working on the translation of that one now. Talk to you tomorrow. This is amazing.

Often times, tone is lost via text message, but in this case the excitement of the search for answers shone through. This was the first real excitement James had felt since the fire in Genna, too. He was tired of floundering. This was something entirely new to him and he wasn't sure what he could really contribute to the team. On the other hand, he did inadvertently discover the stone that led to the discovery of the cavern, so that was something. James needed to do this. He needed something positive to focus on so he could pull himself out of his funk. It helped that he liked the Professor. They had only known each other for a couple of days, and yet, it felt much longer, such was the comfort that he felt hanging out with Stuart.

As he dozed off, his head and his dreams were filled with visions of Vikings and Jesus, which seemed like an unlikely combination. They morphed into pharaohs and pyramids. Just as Indiana Jones rushed out to avoid the giant rolling boulder that threatened to crush him, James snapped awake.

The early morning, spring sunshine beamed in between the blinds. Though it had seemed to him that he had only slept for moments, he hopped out of bed virtually bursting with energy. He jumped in the shower and got ready for the day, before checking his phone. He had more messages, seven to be precise, from Stuart. The last one had come in at three-thirty in the morning, it simply said, *Come over as soon as you get this.*

James tossed an English muffin into the toaster, pulled it out and munched it dry as he walked next door. He rapped on the door.

"Come in!"

James let himself in and wandered into the living room. Stuart sat at the dining room table, which was covered in papers and books. So was the floor beneath him. Stuart looked every bit like the obsessed academic, still wearing the same dirty clothes that he had worn when he fell through the rock pile into the cave. His hair was disheveled his socks were twisted with one big toe poking out through a hole.

"What's happening, Doc?"

Stuart put one hand up, "Give me a minute." He pointed toward the kitchen, "Coffee is in there." He never looked up from his work during the exchange.

James wandered into the kitchen, "Want me to pour you a cup?"

"That's why I sent you in there."

James found two clean cups and filled them with hot, slightly stale-smelling brew and walked back into the other room and set the Professor's cup on the only clear spot on the table. He could see notes and sketches of symbols covering every page.

"It all looks Greek to me."

"That's it!" cried the Professor as he scrambled to find a specific note amidst the mound of paper. He found what he was looking for and filled in an empty space. "You see, it was Omega. Sometimes the answer to the riddle of translation is so simple that you gloss right over it. Overcomplicating it, unnecessarily."

He finally turned to look at James, "but your innocent quip that it looked like Greek triggered just the connection within my brain that I needed to pull it all together."

"So, what does it say?"

"Well, it's not that easy. There are thirty-seven separate inscriptions, in thirty-one languages that I can tentatively identify. What time is it?" He glanced at his watch, "Good, Fredrick should be in his office before long and he can help me confirm those."

The harried Professor dug through the pile again and came out with two sheets of crinkled paper. He pulled his glasses from the top of his head back down onto his nose and cleared his throat, "Okay, the *Aramaic* one turns out to be, *Old Aramaic*. The language of several centuries before Jesus' time. It later morphed and replaced *Hebrew* as the language of the common people throughout the middle east, though *Hebrew* remained the primary language amongst the Jewish religious, government and upper-class crowd, it is likely that Jesus and his followers spoke *Aramaic*. Based on the intricacies of the script I would guess this version of the language came from the 8th or 9th century BCE. But, of course, keep in mind that doesn't mean the engraving itself is that old, only the script that was used. Think of it as a font, on your Word document. You might be typing in an Old English font, but you are typing it now, in the present. There is no measure of age associated with it. Are you with me so far?"

"Pretty much... I think. The language used is twenty-nine hundred years old, but we don't know when it was put there."

"Correct. Give or take a hundred years or so. But

that inscription says this:" He spun the paper around and placed it before James.

Seek the golden site and see the vast world in a whole new light.

James read it, and read it again. "What does it mean?"

"I don't know, yet. And of course, *site* could also be building or edifice, and *vast* could be big or wide, but I feel pretty confident in the message. Translation in dead languages is often more interpretation than literal translation, but I was a biblical archaeologist for most of my career. This is one language that I feel pretty confident in. I could try a few more, but it would take me days. These others are the reason we are going to go see Fredrick. He has a gift. Let me go change, then we'll go."

The half-hour drive to Boise State University's campus was majestic as Spring brought fresh blooms to trees and gardens and fresh growth to the many farms along the route, the rolling hills were sprawling green carpets, though snow-capped peaks still shone in the distance. Of course, neither James nor the Professor noticed Spring's bounty, as their minds were occupied by distant lands and distant times.

The Professor broke the silence, "Did I tell you

about the theory that two of my former students came up with the other day?"

"No, not that I recall. You said something about them finding Runes, or actually NOT finding them."

"Right, they're the same two, Michael and Samantha. Anyway, they have this theory that Lewis & Clark were secretly searching for Cibola whilst carrying out the mapping and exploration of the Northwest Territories. I thought it was madness and desperation, but..."

"What's Cibola?"

"Do you remember your high school History courses? Most of them talked about the explorers Cortez and Coronado, at least." He waited for a nod before continuing. "Francisco Vasquez de Coronado was chasing the Spanish myth of the Seven Cities of Gold. El Dorado is the most well-known in the South American version of the Myth, but Cibola was another of the Cities of Gold suspected to be in the New Mexico Territory. There are other similar myths around Portugal and one of Moorish origin if I remember it right. Coronado did, in fact, conquer a village called Cibola in New Mexico, around 1540, but there were no riches to be found. Then another native supposedly told him about another 'City of Gold' called, Quivira that was somewhere in Kansas or Missouri, I can't remember. At any rate, Coronado chased his tail and came up empty again."

He paused and took a pull of his coffee, "So, Michael and Samantha found some document, a personal letter, written by James Madison where he complained about how poorly the treasury was holding up, the new country was going broke as it attempted to become a real country. Anyway, he made a single statement that got their attention, he said *'If only Thomas' search party had been successful.'* Well, they did some digging and found that while Jefferson had never commissioned an expedition to the New Mexico Territory, there was a very famous one just a little to the North that also spent an entire winter in Missouri on its way west."

"Lewis & Clark?"

"Very good. So now, in the same week we find an unknown letter from Clark in a strange mountain complex of some sort. But not only that, we find a stone carving near it, in *Old Aramaic* nonetheless that mentions a *golden site*. While the search may have been farfetched, Michael and Samantha's theory suddenly doesn't sound so outlandish."

"Are you saying we may have found one of the Seven Cities of Gold?"

"No, no. I am merely suggesting that they may have been looking for Cibola when they came across this place, whatever it is, and shut it down. There are too many coincidences to rule it out, anyway. Plus, did you see any gold there?"

"Well, no." James replied sheepishly.

"Here we are. And don't mention Cibola to anyone here, or anyone at all. If they think I am searching for a City of Gold, I will lose all credibility and therefore any help that they can offer. Academia is famous for its ability to shun someone who disturbs the happy balance that they have between the History that they have sold for all of these years and the reality of what actually happened."

"Okay."

They walked across the perfectly manicured lawn and passed rows and rows of bicycles locked to corrals, though very few actual students, on their way to the towering dark brick and glass Arts & Science Building. They made their way to the fifth floor, then wound back to the far back corner of the building where Stuart knocked on an unlabeled door.

"Enter."

Stuart pushed his way through the door, into a rather small office loaded with book cases and filing cabinets. Beyond the first row of clutter they made their way to the desk, behind which sat a small-statured grey-haired man in spectacles. His bright yellow Hawaiian shirt was a contradictory statement to an otherwise dull office.

"Hello, Fredrick."

"Stuart, it's been a while. What have you been up to?"

"Stuck in exile... until now."

Fredrick knew much of the story, he was one of the few people in academia that Stuart had trusted to tell... most of it at least.

"Hi, I'm James Angeline." James interrupted awkwardly.

"I'm sorry, I should have introduced my associate."

"I'm Dr. Schmidt, but most people call me Fredrick." He reached out and the two shook hands.

"Well, I don't suppose you came by to shoot the breeze. What have you got for me?"

Stuart reached into his leather satchel and pulled out a manila folder. "We found something very unusual. You know me, if I say it's strange, well, you know... This find is so unexpected that I can only imagine that it must be fake, and yet, everything about it is real. Even some other evidence nearby. Here, take a look."

He handed the file to Fredrick, who flipped the file open and looked at the first photo for what seemed like minutes, but was, in fact, only seconds. Then he flipped through the rest in relatively rapid fashion. "Looks like some sort of waypoint marker. I thought you were stuck here in the U.S.?"

"The America's, not just America, but yes, my

work is local."

Fredrick looked at James, "So, it was you that found this?" not understanding what Stuart meant.

"Well, yes, actually."

"Let me guess... Turkey? Or Cairo?"

"No, why would you guess Turkey?"

"Istanbul, or rather, Constantinople would have been one of the only places that had enough trade routes streaming through it to get such a variety of tongues. Though Egypt continues to surprise us."

James looked at Stuart, uncertain as to how much to share. These were not his people; this was not his circle. When Stuart offered nothing, he replied, "You're a little less than one-hundred-fifty miles from it."

"From which one, Istanbul?"

Stuart now interceded, "No, Fredrick. From here. We found it about one-hundred-fifty miles north of here."

"Hogwash." He reacted, certain that this was a prank. When neither of them fessed-up, he stood up. "Impossible."

He reached over and turned on his LED desk lamp then sat back down to look at the first photo again. He swung a lighted magnifying glass over to get a close-up view before he looked up again. "This isn't a joke?"

Both men simply shook their heads as they gave

him time to come to terms with the unusual find. After a few minutes, Stuart broke the silence, "There are thirty-seven inscriptions, Fredrick and as far as I can tell, at least thirty-one different languages."

"Twenty-nine, two of those are different dialects of the same language. I am baffled, not so much by the languages, but by the time periods. Well, and of course, by the location but that's your concern, not mine. But there are languages here that span several millennia, many of them virtually dead."

"Look Fredrick, I know this is an odd piece. But I think this will hold information about something else that I found, which I am not able to discuss just yet. So, I know that there is little context for you to work with on the translation, but I have a feeling that if you work them one at a time, they will provide their own context. I will worry about authenticating it later, right now I just need to know what it says. Can you do that for me? Can you text me as you finish each one?"

Fredrick smiled, "Well, it's either work on this, or suffer another dreadful Staff Luncheon. You know how I feel about those." He winked at them before his eyes reverted back to the picture in his hands.

"Thank you. I owe you one." Stuart said.

"Thirty-seven, you owe me thirty-seven."

Fredrick's German heritage reared its head.

Angeline laughed, "Well, I already did the *Old Aramaic* one, and another is simply two letters, *W* and *C* as if they are initials. We'll call it thirty-five then."

"Well, I will need to confirm your competence in *Aramaic*." He retorted, only half-jokingly.

As the two men turned to leave, Fredrick called out, "Did you find gold? That's the one word that jumps out at me that is common to many of these."

"Not a nugget, we found something, I haven't figured out what it is yet, but it isn't gold."

When the two men left, Fredrick looked uncertainly at the phone on his desk. He didn't want to betray his friend, especially this one. He had already lost so much due to politics and greed. But Fredrick had debts and some kinds of debts absolutely must be repaid.

He dialed a number from a card taped to the side of his monitor and held his breath. The line clicked and beeped as Fredrick imagined the signal being bounced around the world.

It wasn't. Instead it was channeling through a line-scrubber before being put through an encryption protocol so state of the art that it would have made the NSA blush... had they known of its existence.

"Yes." A highly-refined male voice finally

answered.

Fredrick stumbled, "um, yes. Sir, this is Dr. Schmidt at Boise State. You had inquired about some specific information. Well some of it has just landed in my lap."

"Tell me, this line has been secured."

Fredrick proceeded to tell the man about his encounter with Stuart and his friend. Though he conveniently left out the fact that Stuart was a good friend. No reason to cause this man to doubt his loyalty. Unfortunately, at this particular time his loyalty went to the highest bidder. And the man that he was more terrified of.

"Very well. How long will it take you to translate the stone?"

"Well, the scope of these unusually combined phrases makes it..."

"How long?" the man's impatience was crystal clear.

"Several will be done in the next few hours, the rest could take a few days."

"I want to be copied on what you find. Thirty-six hours. I will pick up the translations tomorrow afternoon at four-thirty. Do not disappoint me."

Fredrick looked at the phone as the line clicked dead. The dread in the pit of his gut told him that he had just made a terrible mistake.

He's coming here, personally? That can't be good.

CHAPTER TWELVE

August 25th, 1805

The Hasabi villagers finished their meal, which was immediately followed by a strange ritualized dance-trance that lasted for several hours before the drums stopped beating and the exhausted villagers retired to their huts. Will and Meriwether observed the entire scene from the relative safety of the gazebo that they had once been lashed to. The villagers still seemed wary of them, and once the rituals started Lewis & Clark felt it would be much too dangerous to be out amongst them, one never knew what they might decide to sacrifice during the ceremony. Plus, the two captives wanted to simply blend into the background and let everyone forget that they were here. That was part of the plan.

At one point in the evening, they had fallen back beyond the gazebo and were sitting together leaning against the side of one of the huts that seemed to be used for storage or something. During the late afternoon they had noticed quite a few of the villagers seemed to come and go from that particular hut. At any rate, it was the closest hut and the easiest way for them to begin blending into the background and shadows, whilst not drawing attention by being gone. No, if they simply slinked off into the jungle someone would notice, but easing their way into the shadows of the night might just make them invisible to their captors even before they actually took off. It also gave them a great deal of time to let their eyes adjust to ever darker conditions; they would need their night vision to survive.

Though the Hasabi guards hadn't taken part in the rituals and they had made themselves scarce during the festivities. At one point, Tmboku came running to the gazebo, presumably looking for the two of them. However, once he located them sitting innocently against the hut, he sighed and returned to wherever he had come from.

Once they had been left alone for quite a while, Will leaned over and whispered, "I think I have it all worked out; a way to stop Andres and his madness, free these people, and just maybe get us home. Here's what we need to do..."

Will took Lewis through the whole plan and had him repeat it back to him, twice. "Remember, if I don't make it to the rendezvous, you haul your ass back to the portal and find a way to shut it down from the other side. Understood?"

With an affirmative nod from his long-time friend, Will slipped into the jungle.

Though Will grew up slinking through the forests of Virginia, he had learned much about silent stalking from his Indian companions over the last couple of years. Those lessons allowed him to move quickly through the jungle without even rustling a leaf. There were only a few uncertainties that could jeopardize his plan, and the biggest unknown was this; running through the jungle in the dark without any idea if predators were waiting, or whether the indigenous people of Hasabi had set traps in the jungle as a means of protecting the path. Both were strong possibilities that would likely end in his demise, one way or another.

He rushed through the jungle, parallel to the pathway they had taken earlier in the evening, with his senses tingling at maximum intensity searching out any of the plethora of dangers that faced him: traps, snakes, tigers, panthers, guards and any number of unknown variables. He could see that the torches that had lit the pathway earlier were no longer burning. He had already jumped over one tripwire when he saw the next obstacle in his path. A long dark snake slid through a gap that Will needed to take. Will slowed to let it pass by before continuing. Instead, the snake sensed his presence and reared up into a striking position before it flared out its hood. Will had become accustomed to dealing with rattlers and water moccasins in the United States, but he knew that cobras were universally either feared or worshiped. He didn't have time for either. He picked up his pace and as he reached what he estimated as the striking distance for the cobra, Will leaped through the air with a rolling twist and as he passed over it his hand shot forward and snatched the bewildered snake by the neck, then hit the ground rolling. Keeping a firm grip on the reptile, he let the momentum roll him right back up to his feet and kept moving, the snake's tail dragging in their wake.

He had to keep moving, for the noise of his barrel roll could have attracted the attention of someone, he needed to get some distance. He suddenly saw some flicker light ahead, which caused him to slow down. The change in velocity allowed the cobra to get his tail up and tried to wrap it around Will's wrist. Will fought it off with his left hand, unwinding the tail while edging closer to the lighted clearing. It didn't appear to be nearly as well-lit as it had been earlier, which he took as a stroke of good luck... or divine assistance, either way that eased this next part just a bit. As he approached the edge of the clearing, he could see that there were only four torches now, each held by one of the four of Andres' personal guards that he could see along the perimeter, including one mere steps away from him. There was a possibility that there were more guards in the shadows, but Will suspected that given the king's arrogance and hubris security was less about quality and more about show. He also suspected that he would know that answer in about thirty seconds.

Will knew that holding torches should kill the guards' night vision, therefore he only needed to create a small path through the shadows and could possibly go undetected. His other option was to take out the guard in front of him, and his torch. That would leave only three visually-impaired guards and a wider path through the shadows.

Clark deftly stepped up behind the guard and holding the cobra like a garrote, swung the snake's tail around the man's neck from one side, then tossed the head around the other side. The man instantly dropped his spear and screeched as he tried to get the primally agitated creature off of him. Will snagged the spear before it hit the ground, then grabbed the torch from his hand and swung it toward his elaborate robes setting them ablaze before dropping it and racing across the shadow space between him and the house. Out of his peripheral vision he could see the other three guards, and their torches, converging not on him, but on their fallen comrade.

Will hustled up the now darkened steps and right up to the front door. He placed his ear against it and listened for the sound of any voices that might have been alerted by the screaming of the guard. He heard nothing.

He eased the door open and stepped inside. This part of his plan also had two bits of uncertainty. The first was that he wasn't sure whether the albino tiger was normally chained-up in the entryway, or whether it was only brought up for an intimidation factor for Andres' guests last night. The low growl emanating from the left side of the room answered that. The second bit of uncertainty was whether Will survived the encounter.

Will silently edged his way along the wall toward the majestic beast. He heard it climb to its feet as he got closer, it let out a short snort of warning followed by more of the low rumbling. This was the moment of truth.

Will had always had a way with animals, even as a kid running around the hills and farms of Virginia.

He could calm wild horses, unruly pigs, coyotes, and even bobcats by looking them in the eye and talking to them. It was something of a gift. Of course, the difference between a bobcat and a full-grown albino tiger was monumental. It was a gamble.

"Hi big guy, remember me?" He cooed softly and non-threateningly. He was also concerned that the darkness would make it difficult for him to make real eye contact, but decided that, for most cats, their night-vision was far superior to that of humans. So, while he may not be able to see well, he had to believe and act as if he could. The cat would see either way. Calmness, confidence and faith were what this required.

"Wow, what a big beautiful beast you are." He took another step.

"How can he keep you confined like this? You should be free and powerful." He took another step and then crouched down onto a knee, his head even and level with the beast's. Another growl emitted from its throat.

Will simply said, "Shhhhhhhhhhhhhh... It's okay big guy. It's okay."

He knew this was the moment that it could all go horribly wrong. The cat stepped closer, still grumbling, but not acting overly aggressive either. The tiger now stood nearly nose to nose with Will, sniffing and growling. Will moved his left hand ever so slowly toward the cat, above its head and gave a small scratch behind its ear before continuing backward. Blindly, his fingers found the pin and gave a gentle pull. It moved a bit, not enough but a bit. Throughout this process Will's eyes never left those of the tiger. To break that connection now would be suicidal. Of course, one could argue that this whole plan was suicidal.

"Good boy," he whispered as he gave the pin one more quick tug. The collar and the chain fell to the floor with a loud clank causing the tiger to flinch. The flinch gave Will pause; fear that the spell he had the cat under was broken by the sound of the chain hitting the floor. He slowly backed away and stood up. The tiger matched his steps and when Will had stood up tall, it leaned in and pushed its head into his thigh. Will scratched it behind the ear, gently at first, then more deeply. The tiger growled. But it was obvious to Will that it was a roar of gratitude.

"Come on, boy!" Will whispered with a bit more urgency. He walked over to the closed door to the dining room. The tiger pranced at his side.

Suddenly he heard voices through the door, one of which was terribly familiar.

"Oh, shut up, Zanzibar! Somebody, take that tiger outside!! Chain him to a tree or something. If he keeps up this racket all night, he will end up being dinner tomorrow night." Andres railed in English, before switching to the Hasabi tongue. Other voices responded in what sounded like gibberish to Clark.

Will wasn't certain how, but at that moment he would have sworn that he felt Zanzibar tense up as Andres mentioned having him for dinner. Perhaps, it was only the sound of Andres' voice that did it. Will took that as his cue to open the double doors wide, catching the looks on the faces of the three men morph from surprise, to recognition, to terror all within the span of two seconds. Will stepped forward, spear at the ready. Zanzibar needed no weapons.

The cat launched headlong at the indigenous man near him, screams ensued for a brief moment. Then the screams of fear came from Andres and the other guard in the room as they saw the first man ripped open in a single claw-swipe before the tiger went for his throat.

Andres spun on his heel and shrieked back toward his quarters. Zanzibar, glanced at Will, then bounded off in pursuit, bowling over the other man on his way past. Zanzibar had a score to settle with Andres. Will finished off the downed man with a spear-thrust through the chest.

An enormous roar reverberated through the dwelling, Will silently wished his new friend good luck. He rushed over to the throne and tested it to see how heavy it was. Will silently said a prayer of thanks that it wasn't nearly as dense and heavy as it would have been had it been made of gold. No, the mysterious alloy was significantly lighter.

Will had realized during dinner that the reason for Andres' longevity, his 'immortality' wasn't because he was a god. His lack of aging came from the powers embedded in the golden, flowing metal from the portal site. Take away the chair and Andres' might just become a killable, if he survived Zanzibar's rage.

Will flipped the chair over his shoulder and began running awkwardly toward the front door, "Zanzibar, Come on!" He didn't know if the cat would come, but he might be of help. Not waiting to find out, Will bolted down the front steps and into the clearing. Two of the guards had returned to their posts, but the cobra-stricken man and the fourth were unaccounted for. Their absence left a fairly dark gap between the two guards which became Will's target path. It wasn't nearly as graceful as his approach to the building on arrival had been, but he was carrying a King's throne, so perhaps graceful wasn't to be expected.

He tore into the jungle at nearly the same place that he had exited it just a dozen minutes ago. The sound of the chair legs crashing against leaves and branches was loud enough to attract the notice of the guards and he soon heard numerous calls, clicks and yells as the two tried to rally the rest of the warriors. Despite that, he heard nobody else crashing through behind him. That gave him hope that perhaps, the plan might actually work. He hoped with all of his might that Meriwether had been able to break away and find the rendezvous point. Meriwether, too, had grown up in Virginia, though many more of his days there had been spent reading and studying than racing through the forest like Will had.

He continued busting through the jungle toward the rendezvous, twice the chair snagged and was ripped out of his hands but overall, he felt like he was making good time. Suddenly he saw torches blazing downhill and to the right of him. Just a couple, but he knew more would be coming. He needed to be quieter, but with the throne, that would slow him down considerably. Which was more important speed or sound? In his mind both were equally important. But if he had to choose, then in this moment, stealth was more important.

Will veered left a bit to distance himself from the pursuers that he could see, but also crawled to a slow walk so as not to disturb any of the fauna or flora in this deep dark place. He made it about one hundred yards, then realized that he was very near to passing the rendezvous. He stopped and listened for sounds around him., searching for both Lewis and the Hasabi warriors.

Suddenly an enormous explosion blew the hatch roof off of one of the huts, Will didn't know which one, but he was certain that people throughout the entire kingdom would now be looking for him. He began moving again and stumbled upon a small clearing, really only about fifteen feet across, but he hadn't expected to have to break cover this soon. He had believed that they would only have to break cover in the final dash to the portal. He came to a complete stop at the edge of the clearing; his senses screaming that this was a bad place to be. It would take him awhile to get around it, but that's what his gut was telling him to do.

Something moved at the far side of the clearing. A man stepped out onto the path. No, it was two men, one in front of the other.

"Will, it's a trap!" Meriwether yelled before Tmboku tightened his forearm around his throat and choked silence into him. Lewis struggled. Will stepped forward, the chair still on his shoulder.

"Okay, Tmboku. Okay." he raised one hand in a sign of submission.

Will could just make out the tripwire that the warrior was trying to lure him toward, but since the bait that he was using was Will's best friend he couldn't exactly run away. He would have to let himself trigger the trap. His eyes followed the tripwire to get a sense of what the trap might be. To his left, the line terminated at a stake in the ground, thus, he thought it was likely that whatever the primitive trap might be would spring from the right side. Unless, of course, it triggered something above, or below for that matter.

"I give up. Okay? Ease up on him." He stalled knowing that Tmboku couldn't understand him. He hefted the throne up higher on his right shoulder and gripped it tightly as he took a cautious step forward. The metal leg of the chair flowed and bent between his fingers as he squeezed tight and took the final step and tripped the wire.

The bushes along the right side of the clearing exploded as a flurry of darts launched through the air. Several slammed into the throne, but since Will was only half a step into the kill zone, the majority of them passed harmlessly into the other side of the forest. One, however, must have found its mark, as a scream went out and a torch bearing guard collapsed a dozen or two yards from where Will still stood.

Tmboku had seen enough. Enraged he threw Lewis to the ground and held his tomahawk high as he raced toward Clark to finish the job himself. Will saw it coming but his only defensive weapon was the throne itself and it made him far too slow to respond to this threat. *It was a good try. We almost made it.*

"Run, Meri! Now!" He shouted as he accepted his own fate. He had done all he could.

Just as Tmboku reached striking distance the bushes just to the left of Will exploded. A light flash blew between the two and Tmboku screamed a blood curling scream as Zanzibar ducked the tomahawk and drove straight through the warrior's chest. Powerful paws swiped this way and that, leaving Tmboku flayed and beaten in a matter of seconds. The cat was in full predator mode as he circled the center of the clearing searching for any more threats. Finding none, he pranced over to Will and, again, begged for his ears to be rubbed.

"You saved me, my friend. Thank You." He said to the muscular beast, who simply nuzzled into his thigh again.

But Will understood what it meant: *We saved each other.*

He rubbed and scratched Zanzibar's head. "Good luck to you, my friend. I wish I could take you back with me, but you will be better off here."

Will looked toward where Meri, had been. Thankfully, he had taken his advice and run. Meri was far from cowardly, in fact, he was very brave to have undertaken the expedition. But despite having served in the military, Meriwether wasn't nearly as battle-hardened as Will. He was more of a supply and logistics soldier, while Will had been in the trenches. They made a good pair, each balancing and complimenting the other's strengths and weaknesses.

Will rebalanced the throne on his shoulder and took off toward the cavern and the portal. One his way through the clearing he had to high-step another tripwire, avoiding yet another volley of darts, presumably poisonous ones. He continued through the jungle, now just meters from the road that they had been led down when they had first been captured. He noticed signs of Lewis' run through the jungle; broken limbs and branches, displaced groundcover, clear footprints. It was lucky that nobody else seemed to be tracking them. He didn't know what had happened to the remaining warriors, but since Tmboku had fallen, all of the torches had disappeared.

He also didn't know for certain what the status of Andres David, the now fallen king. But he suspected that, if Zanzibar hadn't finished the job, he would be searching desperately for his 'magic' chair. For unless Will was mistaken, by the end of the day Ol' Andres was going to start feeling his age.

He picked up his pace, and Zanzibar stayed close to him despite their goodbyes. Finally, he converged with the road. As he stepped out of the bush he came to a sudden stop. A growl sounded from right behind him. At the entrance to the winding tunnel which led to the portal stood eight of the guardian warriors. Tmboku's warriors. This time, however, they showed no outward signs of aggression. In fact, once they made eye contact with Will, each one of them kneeled on one knee and bowed their heads. It was difficult for Will to decipher whether the act was a sign of submission or a sign of respect. He speculated that it was a combination of the two.

He nodded his head at the one kneeling slightly in front of the others, presumably the new leader of the pack. He wanted to say something to them, but knew they wouldn't understand. Andres still pricking the back of Will's mind gave him a reason to say it anyway. And pantomime.

He pointed to the throne, then pointed toward the 'castle' before putting his fingers to his mouth in an eating motion. "The King is all yours."

He turned into the cave. Zanzibar followed him.

There was nobody in the cavern, hopefully Meri was on the other side searching for a way to disable the portal. Will set the chair down.

"You can't come with me big guy. But you can stay here if you want. It's big and spacious and will protect you from the rain."

Though he knew that the wild beast didn't need it, Will ripped the padding off of the chair, tossed the darts that were sticking out of it into the corner, out of the way, and fashioned a makeshift bed for his friend and savior, in front of the machine. If nothing else, it was a bit of security until they figured out how to disable the portal.

"Come on, boy." He patted the bed, signaling for the tiger to lay down. He did, with a groan, then promptly rolled over on his back demanding that his belly be rubbed. After a few moments of scratching, Will stood, picked up the remains of the throne and walked back up the ramp and through the portal.

Again, he felt nothing but a change in the air and a quick flash, instantly he was walking down the ramp again and his ears were assaulted with the sound of the rushing water. He was back.

CHAPTER THIRTEEN

May 8th, 2019

"I think this is it!" Dr. Angeline exclaimed after handing a box down to James from atop the sturdy steel shelves in his storage unit.

It was the thirteenth time that the Professor had made the claim, but James saw that there was only one more box on the shelf that they hadn't checked, so he figured the chances were an even fifty-fifty. Filthy, sweaty, and covered in dust the professor climbed down the ladder as James cut through the tape with his pocket knife. Stuart sidled up to him and when he had it open began rifling through the contents.

"I just need this one more thing."

James looked over at the back of the SUV through the roll-up door of the unit. It was packed full of boxes and equipment. "I'm glad it's just one more, not sure we'd get much more in there."

Stuart ignored him, "Ah ha! Here it is!" he exclaimed as he held up a gadget that resembled a stud finder for your home.

"Do you want to decorate while we're there? That stud finder should be able to find the giant, uncovered metal beams, that's for sure." James joked.

"It's not a stud finder. This is a satellite driven tool that does a number of things, like give you accurate coordinates, date, time, humidity, elevation, and a bunch more. It is a very handy tool for documenting a dig site. It should even work in the cavern, though I haven't tested that."

"I wonder if it can find us lunch? I'm starving."

"Okay, okay. I think we are done here, anyway."

James could see his wheels still spinning, not sure if he had everything that he would need. Of course, James had no idea what was entailed at an archeological dig site, this was his first one. His gauge as to whether they had everything was simply related to how full the SUV was. It seemed like enough. The Professor had made a good point though, the site was so isolated and such a distance away, it made sense to take whatever they could, just in case.

Finally, the professor relented, "Okay, let's go grab something to eat, then get on the road."

After they ate, Stuart tossed the keys to James. "You drive, so I can get some work done on the way."

A few minutes later they were headed north. Moments after that the passenger side dashboard was covered with photos, paper, and files. The Professor was viewing them through an oversized magnifying glass, though the scans were already enlarged. With a notebook open on his lap and pencil tucked behind his ear, he fit all of the stereotypes James had of academics, except for the fact that he was also adventurous. Perhaps that sense of adventure was what separated field archaeologists from the campus-bound academics.

This was all new to James Augustine. He was a word guy and a political message creator, not an archaeologist. Even so, he could feel the excitement building as they got closer. He had always been a history geek; he just never knew that he would be a part of something like this.

"Why are you working on translations? I thought that is why we went to see Fredrick." James asked, breaking the silent monotony.

"Do you remember when I told you that translating older languages is more like interpretation than it is literal translation?"

"Yes."

"Well that also means you're better off having more than a single translation, by a single linguist. It is better to have multiple variants and therefore a better composite at the end. First rule of translation is to have more than one translator."

"What's the second rule of translation?"

"Never give them the whole picture. Always hold something back."

"Why is that?"

"If they have the whole story and the translations these discoveries have a way of quickly becoming someone else's discovery. I have seen it happen too many times, driven by greed. The Antiquities Black Market is a multi-billion-dollar industry. Too many people in the archaeological support community are on retainer to the wealthy, while field archaeologists struggle to get grants to fund a dig. It can be a dirty business, especially in the middle east."

"But you don't struggle to get grants."

"No, not anymore. But that's a payoff for having to quash my most significant discovery. It feels like hush-money, and I suppose it is. But now we have the means to really process this site, so I suppose it was worth it. This is going to be special."

"Obviously, it is some type of machinery. What do you think it did?"

"I am hoping that some of these translations from the Waypoint Stone will help us figure it out. Whatever it is, people from all over the world have been making pilgrimages to it for a few thousand years at least. The question is *why*? Of course, how is also a question that I haven't answered yet. None of the rest of the world seemed to know North America was here until the 15th century, so how did all these people travel here so secretly that there weren't even whispers of a new continent until around a thousand years ago."

Stuart's phone beeped and dinged indicating that a text had arrived. He looked and saw that he had three texts from Fredrick. Angeline opened the first:

I hadn't noticed these before, but there are two English (Roman) letters scratched
onto the stone. They look to be newer and more scratched-in than carved-in.
The letters are W and C. I don't know what to make of them- More to follow

Augustine & Angeline looked at each other and, in unison, said, "William Clark!"

"Something about the place must have made enough of an impact on him to justify etching his initials into the stone, even though he didn't document the discovery anywhere else," Stuart opined, as he clicked on the next text.

Attached was a picture of one of the phrases, followed by the text:

The hieroglyphs translate roughly to:
A golden pyramid, a flash of light and a whole new world fills my eye.
Even the gods don't know from where to here. (or possibly from whence we came)

Stuart copied the translation into his notebook before clicking on the final text.

The runic translation is:
The gilded-gates to Valhalla begin the journey of eternal life, though strange
lands cloud the way there is a path to Oden's sanctuary.

Stuart copied it down too. "Three translations, each mention gold and refer to some sort of gateway. The thing is, I didn't see anything gold. Did you?"

"Maybe it doesn't refer to our site at all, maybe it is something else entirely. But with what you said about your students and the seven cities of gold that makes an awful lot of references to gold to dismiss.

We might just be missing something. Once we light up the chamber maybe we'll get some answers. There might even be other chambers in the cave."

"But that's just the thing. If that many people had come to the site from distant lands, and signed the Waypoint Stone, what are the chances that there would be any gold left. You would think that the first one would have looted it. But centuries of travelers mention the same thing."

James glanced at the rear-view mirror. There was a small gray Toyota SUV behind them. He had seen the same car when they had fueled up in Horseshoe Bend. "Stuart, did you bring any weapons in all of this stuff?"

"No, why?"

"I think we're being followed."

Angeline whipped his head around and looked over the load and out the back window. "Nobody knows we've found anything. Well, nobody but Fredrick, anyway. Probably just a coincidence. Lots of people take this route from Boise to McCall every day. Either way, that little cabin restaurant is coming up on the right, let's take a bathroom break and see if they just drive on by, or not. Then we'll know."

It was a practical test. James knew that he was probably being over protective of their site, but his gut instinct had served him well in recent years. He wasn't prone to paranoia normally, especially since he got sober. In the depths of his alcoholism he saw shadows everywhere. He didn't like the suddenly familiar feeling.

A couple of miles up, the cabin appeared. James slowed and pulled past it into the open gravel parking lot and rolled to a stop. They watched through the back window as the SUV continued up the highway with nary a glance.

"Okay, all this talk of gold just has me paranoid, I guess." James admitted.

The two got out, stretched their legs, and took a quick bathroom break before re-embarking on their journey. The Professor went back to work on his translations. He quickly confirmed one of Fredrick's translations, then went back to the petroglyph that he had been working on earlier. He had spent much of the winter studying the local Native American folklore and languages, but didn't have much experience with trying to decipher them. With a couple reference checks and a google search he believed he had this one figured out.

The ancient ancestors light the way to the spirit world, cross the doorway but beware the evil spirits that seek despair in this world and the next.

"Well, that's not terribly uplifting."

"It's interesting, though. Since I have been studying the local tribes, I have seen many writings that talk about ancestors, but I have never come across one with redundant descriptors like this on. 'Ancient ancestors' seems to show an unusual reverence to the ancestors of the ancestors. Of course, this isn't my specialty. I could be reading into it."

"There is definitely something that we are missing. All of these quotes talk about gates, gateways, doorways or some similar description. But all we saw was an interesting room filled with equipment of some sort. No gateways to other realms, no doors."

Caught up in conversation, neither of the men noticed a very familiar gray SUV pull out of a side-street and fall in behind them.

"I wonder if it is more of a spiritual gateway or door. Perhaps the place when it's operational was more of a religious or spiritual experience. Perhaps it induces hallucinations, like the local natives can fall into in sweat lodges or other extreme meditative experiences. People have been known to make extraordinary pilgrimages to religious sites throughout history, whether to Mecca, Stonehenge, or to Tibet, man has traveled far and wide for the experience. Maybe the machine creates certain wavelengths that stimulate the brain in such a way."

"A God Machine?"

"Whether it is true or not, if people believe it is, then they will go to great lengths to commune with their God. That's why I find it so interesting that people from so many places and times– and presumably different faiths- have journeyed here to the center of what was thought to be an unknown wildland."

"I understand having such a spiritual experience, but how on earth would they have been able to keep it secret over several thousand years? Not to mention the fact that the machine looks more futuristic than ancient. We need to figure out how it works. The puzzle pieces don't fit. And what about the consistent mention of gold?"

James was so wrapped up in thought that he almost missed the turn off of the highway, but he braked hard and exited. At the intersection he turned left and followed the road that ran along the edge of the Salmon River. As he rounded a bend, he noticed the familiar front end of a vehicle behind them.

"I think that SUV is behind us again. I can't be sure, but it sure looks the same."

"Ok, just keep going to the trailhead. I have an idea."

"So do I." James said as he pulled his everyday carry, his EDC, from his hip beneath the seatbelt and placed it on the center console where it was more accessible, should he actually need it. The Smith & Wesson Shield 9mm wouldn't be great if they were faced with any real firepower, as he only had the 8 rounds that were loaded into the magazine, but at least it was something.

"I didn't even know you carried."

"I suppose that's why it's called concealed carry."

"We always had good local security at dig sites in the middle east, I never imagined that we would need it here, especially since nobody knows about this find yet."

"Like you said, it's probably a coincidence. But I don't like it."

The road wound along the path of the Salmon, but the constant winding meant that James never again really got a glimpse of the vehicle behind them. Eventually he turned off, toward the trailhead. When they reached it, he stopped. "Okay, what now."

"Switch seats, I'll drive for this part."

They got out and switched places. "If that is the same one, it was one of those compact, like a RAV4 or something. They have little to no ground clearance. One of the advantages to having a Range Rover is that I can take this thing almost anywhere."

With that, Stuart drove around the trailhead barrier and continued up the path until it got too narrow to continue. He stopped and switched it into four-wheel drive.

"Hold on tight, this will be a bit wonky."

He eased the Range Rover off the path and down what was once a riverbank before reaching the rocky riverbed. Moving at a slow crawl he maneuvered back and forth to more even sections, but even those were like a poorly laid cobblestone road littered with potholes. Some sections were obviously where rapids had once been, with larger stones jutting out and dropping into deep holes. James thought briefly that a monster truck might be the only way to pass through those sections, but the Professor's calm, focused crawling kept them moving up the riverbed.

Ten minutes later they had made it to the tunnel opening. He kept on going, driving the SUV right into the cavern.

CHAPTER FOURTEEN

August 25th, 1805

"Will, you made it!" came a shout across the cavern.

"I had some help. I think the Hasabi won't be after us anymore, but we should shut this thing down before they change their minds. Any idea how?"

Captain Lewis had been staring at the screen with strange symbols moving across it for the last ten minutes. He presumed that there was a way to shut it off from there, but he had no idea what he was looking at. "No, no idea."

"What is the purpose of the river? They must

have built this place here next to the river for a reason. Could it be powering the place somehow?"

"Powering? Nobody knows how to power anything, at least not outside of a science lab anyway. At
the White House, I did once get to see a demon-
stration of one of Alessandro Volta's battery designs.
It could power small devices, but this? No."

"I don't have to understand all that. But I know
in my gut that this river has a purpose. If we can
shut off the water, I think this place will shut down.
Think about the mines we have passed. How many
of them used waterwheels to operate other things?"

"Do you see a water wheel?"

"No, but clearly whoever built this place is far
more advanced than we are."

"What if we just leave it? Let the mystery of the
River of No Return keep people away."

"What if our enemies decide to use the portal to
bring an army into the middle of our country? Most
of our forces are staged along the coast to deter the
English, French and Portuguese. An army attacking
from this direction would claim half the country before we could even mount a resistance." Will
pleaded.

He was right. This device, this portal, even from
what little they knew about it posed a dire security
concern to the country. And personally, their own
security was in jeopardy from the Hasabi, and on

the off-chance that the God-king had survived his encounter with Zanzibar, there was no doubt in his mind that the madman would be out for blood.

"I guess we have no choice, but to try." Meri conceded. "Let's figure out how to get back out of the tunnel and determine what it would take to dam the river."

"Hang on. There is one thing that I want to take care of first." He took the throne over to the edge of the ledge along the cavern wall and put it down near a pile of stones. He picked up the largest one that he thought he could wield with one hand and slammed it down onto an arm of the chair. The metal was, strangely, both firm and malleable causing it to bend awkwardly. He hit it again, this time closer to the unseen ninety-degree join where the arm morphed into the seat support and became a leg of the chair. He hit it again, this time with both hands driving the stone into the metal. Then again, and again. All of the pent-up anger and frustration, that he had buried whilst in the Hasabi kingdom so that he could remain outwardly calm and rational, poured out of him as he took his aggressions out on the God-King's fountain of youth. Eventually, the throne collapsed on itself until it lay beaten and flattened into something much less regal than what it had been. Once his flurry of rage ended, he buried it with the rest of the pile of stones.

"Feel better?" Meri quipped.

"Yeah, I kind of do. That thing is what gave Andres the time and power to virtually enslave those people, and any others who happened to stumble onto the portal. Breeding with the visitors, and feeding the unworthy to the Hasabi. It is purely evil."

They walked back down the stairs and onto the platform beside the river. Toby had found an answer to the question of how they were going to get out. Attached to the end of the now extended rope was a narrow wooden raft, bobbing to and fro. The raft was constructed of four tree trunks lashed together with leather straps. It was about the width of a man's shoulders and twice as long. It was also shallow enough that if they laid flat, just maybe they wouldn't get battered by the tunnel ceiling as the raft fought the current going upstream.

"After you... Captain." Will ribbed, this time more with good-nature than the caustic jabs that he had thrown the title before.

Will helped hold the raft steady as Meriwether crawled into position. It would be an awkward journey, pulling on the rope hand-over-hand fighting the current inch by inch. After a few minutes he started to feel movement between his pulls and he realized that Toby must have noticed the line jerking and was now reeling him in like a large Salmon. It was hard going, but infinitely easier than doing it with the drag of his whole body being submerged in the water. After a few minutes, Meriwether emerged into the sunlight. Once he made it to the shore, they sent the raft back down for Will and repeated the process, though it went much faster with both Toby and Meri pulling from upstream.

"It good to see you. I thought Great Spirit of the river may have taken you." Toby gleemed.

"Yes, well, it was closer to that than I would have liked." Lewis replied, staying intentionally vague.

Will took a few minutes to catch his breath after the exertion of the tunnel exodus then looked around. "The question is how do we shut it down? If we simply block the tunnel, this whole canyon will fill up with water, creating who knows what ill effects."

"Shut what down?" Toby asked, trying to be helpful.

Lewis & Clark exchanged a glance, not knowing how far to bring Toby into their confidence, but also knowing that they would need his help. After a nod from Meri, Will replied, "The river, we need to stop the river from flowing into that tunnel."

"The Great Mother makes her own path for the river. What's next, do you want to stop the sun?"

"No, this tributary was man-made. Dark spirits, in there," Will pointed at the tunnel entrance, "make this the river of no return. Bad people. If you want to protect your people from disappearing, we need to close this tributary, probably right at the fork. The Great Mother can then have all the water flow down the Big Water, and take it wherever she wants to take it.

Will had spent more than two years living with and amongst Indian tribes. In negotiations he had learned that he needed to use their own phrasing in discussions and arguments, if you want to persuade them of anything. It was awkward, but it was something he had become proficient in.

"Let's walk back to the fork and see what the terrain is like."

"Sounds good, plus we can stop at the camp and get some dry clothes." Meriwether added.

The three men strode down the path and then followed the riverbank to the campsite. They changed into new britches & shirts, then the three saddled and mounted their horses.

Captain Lewis called out to the solitary soldier at the camp, "Corporal, how much gunpowder do we have here?"

"Just one barrel, Captain. Plus a few smaller pouches."

"Do me a favor, ride back to the base camp and bring five barrels back here, as expeditiously as possible."

"Yes, Sir." He saluted and began to gather his things.

Toby, Will, and Meriwether took off along the river, tracing it back to its origin. The canyon walls closed-in and opened-up several times in the one-mile stretch between camp and the river.

"Do you think five more barrels of gunpowder will be enough?" Will asked.

"I have no idea, but I am sure that the one that's here won't be enough for whatever we decide to do."

"True. It would be nice to have engineers build a proper dam instead, but I assume that's not an option."

"Ha, and wait a year to get materials into place before we even start construction, no. That isn't an option."

"Yeah, I suppose not. Besides, we can't have that many people access the site and hope to keep it secret."

"Not to mention, the Hasabi may change their minds and become aggressive again, especially if Andres David is alive. I still can't believe that he has lived for so long."

"With luck that has come to an end." Will declared resolutely.

Before long they approached the noisy junction of the main river, the Big Water, and the tributary.

The land had flattened out and the canyons had stopped a few hundred yards from the fork.

"I don't see anything out here that we can use to dam it up. We don't have the manpower to haul rock in. This isn't going to work." Meriwether stated flatly.

"I don't like the idea of flooding the canyon, but maybe we just blow the tunnel and see what happens when the water has no outlet."

Will reared his horse around, back and forth several times as he thought, like pacing but on horseback. The musculature of his steed contracted with every step. It made him think of Zanzibar and the combination of grace and power he had, even after the madman had chained the magnificent creature to a wall for his own amusement. Will wished he could have brought the cat back with him, but he knew that would have been as selfish as Andres had been. One thing he had learned from the Indians was the concept of balance. The Great Mother tended to keep things in balance in nature, bringing such an amazing predator from his homeland to here would have greatly upset nature's balance, both here and for Zanzibar himself. No, he needed to stay behind. As Will continued to pace like a chained tiger, something caught his eye.

"Toby, have you ever been up there?" He said

pointing to a rock outcropping near the beginning of the canyon wall.

"Yes, biagwi`yaa` live there, or nearby. I helped one with a damaged wing, years ago, and took it up there to return it to its mother's nest."

"Biagwi`yaa`? I don't know that word."

"Big spirit bird, black body and a white head. I don't know what white man call it."

"Like a hawk?"

Toby shook his head, "Not a hawk. Bigger, stronger, beautiful."

Meriwether interjected, "An eagle!"

Toby nodded, "That is word, Toby forget... Eagle."

Will had tuned them out by now as he studied the outcropping. Despite a complete lack of formal education, he had always been good at visualizing things. Angles and geometry, though he didn't know the terms, always made sense to him. His eyes subconsciously measuring the height of the cliff, the size of the outcropping, the way that it would fall and the width of the tributary at that spot.

"It'll work. Show me how to get up there."

The three took off at a trot and crossed a narrow spot in the tributary before going wide and around to come from the backside of the canyon wall. Upon reaching the soaring cliff, they wound along its edge to the outcropping that overhung the cliff face.

Toby was relieved that there was no longer an eagle's nest in the vicinity. He respected nature, but wasn't sure he could have talked the white men out of doing whatever they were trying to do, had the nest still been here. Still he searched the skies seeking the great bird.

Will jumped off his horse and began examining the outcropping and the area behind it. There was a large seam in the stone that might come in handy, but most of the boulders that were up there were too big to move manually, which meant his plan and the explosives had to be targeted just right for it to drop across the tributary.

"Well, Captain. This seems to be our best shot. Do you have any other thoughts?"

"No, but mark your spots and we'll get those braves to come up with the hand drills and get that going while we wait for Corporal Smith to get back with powder."

Will dug around in his saddlebag for a moment before coming out with a chunk of chalk. He, once again, stood and visualized the angles and the pattern of the fall. Then turned and began scratching chalk marks, each a boot-length apart, in a semicircle roughly along the seam in the stone. He stood back and once again imagined how the explosions would blow and which direction the outcropping would fall. He walked up and added one more mark toward the right side of the formation.

"Okay, that should do it. Let's head back down to camp. Toby, can you get your guys and bring them up here to drill these holes. The Captain and I will go take a look above the tunnel and see if we can figure out how to close that off as well."

With a nod to the affirmative, they headed back to camp. Once there, Will dug his journal out of his saddlebag and flipped to the back. He very carefully ripped the last page out and quickly scribbled out a note then wrapped it in leather skin. He needed to protect it for what he had in mind.

"I am ready Captain. Shall we?"

The two followed the path back past the carved rock and back to the tunnel. Will pointed to the rock far above the maw of the tunnel.

"Do you think we could blow the side down in front of the opening with collapsing the cavern?"

"We can if we don't drill in too deep. The question is, will there be enough fallout to hide the entrance."

"Meri, there is something that I need to do before we blow it. I figure we have at least four or five more hours before Smith gets back with the powder."

"Don't say it."

Will kicked Toby's raft with his foot, "I want to go back in. No, I need to go back in."

"To what end, for God's sake."

"It's just something that I need to do. I need to say goodbye to Zanzibar, and I need to know whether Andres is dead. Then I can leave this place behind me. We still don't even know what it is."

"Look at the wars that have raged just in our lifetime. Man is not ready for whatever this thing is."

Clark nodded in agreement. "Can you pull me back out? Give me forty-five minutes, please."

"I suppose, I do owe you one." Lewis joked.

"Just one? Ha!"

The raft was still attached to the rope from before. They quickly placed it into the water and Will shimmied aboard. This time he wasn't going unarmed or unprepared. He had both his pistols and the note that he had written wrapped in oiled skins; he held them to his chest as Meri began to feed the line out and sent Will back into the cavern.

The ride in was surprisingly smooth atop the raft, a significant change from the slow, jerky exit that they had made earlier. Once he got near the platform Will rolled off the raft and immediately headed for the stairs. He set the note on the machine before unwrapping his pistols and sliding them into his holsters. He loosened himself up by shaking his arms and flexing his legs. He was determined not to be taken by surprise again. Judging by the weaponry that the Hasabi elite warriors had, he suspected none of them had ever seen a gun before. He could use that, fear of the unknown, to even the odds if things went south.

Will took a deep breath and then walked straight up the ramp. A breeze, a flash, and silence greeted him as he walked down the ramp. The silence was nearly immediately broken by a vicious sounding roar.

"It's okay Zanzibar, it's me."

Zanzibar stood up from his throne bed, where he had been busy cleaning his paws, and pranced over to offer the top of his head to Will who obliged with a couple of minutes of scratching and rubbing.

As Will was placating the tiger, he scanned the room. The bodies of two of Andres' personal guards lay bleeding and dead just inside the winding tunnel entrance. "Have you been protecting our escape my friend? Or simply defending your new home?"

"Let's go get some answers."

Will headed for the winding exit, stepping over the bodies as he did so. Once he wound his way through the cavern's seam he stepped out into the night-time jungle. After only two steps on the path, he heard feet hitting the ground. The portal warriors were simply protecting the only thing that they had been raised to protect. They did it with honor.

Will held no malice towards them. When Zanzibar stepped out of the tunnel and stood next to Will, the guards backed off a step or two and opened the way down the path. Will wished he knew how to communicate with the warriors. All he really wanted to know was whether Andres was alive or not. He tried to pantomime his questions, but all he got were either laughs or blank stares in return.

He supposed that the only way that he would find the answer was to head back to the castle and see for himself. With Zanzibar at his side, he headed that direction. They snaked their way through the village, past the gazebo and the cooking area, then wound their way up the pathway through the jungle to the castle. The smell of the night's dinner still hung in the air, Will wondered who had been served, then quickly wished he hadn't had that thought. As he approached the clearing and the castle, he made no effort to keep quiet. The last thing that he wanted to do was to startle the King's Personal Guard, instead he whistled nonchalantly as they stepped off of the path and into the clearing. Though a couple of guards still manned their posts, they made no move to stop him. Will and Zanzibar continued at a brisk, but unrushed pace all the way to the front door. He pulled one of his pistols and cocked the hammer back before he pushed through the door and the entryway. Zanzibar growled when his former place of captivity came into view, but didn't falter as the two made their way through the foyer and into the dining room at the far end. Will stepped through and, with his weapon extended in front of him, cleared both blind corners before proceeding through. Next they came to the kitchen area, just as he stepped into the doorway the pale-skinned young girl was coming into the room from another doorway. She froze instantly, dropping the wooden cup that she had been carrying.

Will suspected that even if she didn't know how to speak English, she could probably understand much of it simply from have been raised in the vicinity of Andres David. He raised his hands, palms out, with the barrel of the gun pointing to the ceiling to show her that he meant her no harm.

"King Andres? Is he alive?"

The girl nodded, then surprised him by waving for them to follow her. They walked through a hallway, turned a corner stopping before a large ornate set of double doors. She stepped aside and waved them forward.

Inside they saw that the room was spacious and open, though dimly lit by three candles set in the form of an equilateral triangle; two in either of the far corners and one at the foot of the intricately carved four-post bed. Lying atop the bedding was Andres, no longer the exuberant thirty-something pseudo-immortal king that he had been, but a shriveled, wizened skeleton of a man, with the wounds from claw marks bleeding through the bandages on his belly. It appeared that the combination of near-fatal injury and the loss of the life-extending throne had caused Andres to age more than seventy years in just the half a day since their last encounter. The stench of decay hung heavy in the air and his breathing, noisy and rattling, seemed labored.

The 'God-King' rolled his head to the side to face them as they approached. "Back already?"

Will nodded. Zanzibar stepped forward and put his front paws on the bed to sniff the old man. He let out a roar, then returned to Will's side certain that Andres was no longer a threat.

"Just kill me." Andres rasped breathlessly. "Finish it."

Will could see that fear had replaced the man's ego, and the resoluteness of his choice to stop suffering. He had lived a very long life. Will briefly wondered if he would have become as jaded and arrogant had he lived more than a century and a half. He hoped not, but life was hard enough as it was, enduring four or five normal lifetimes could definitely change a man. What Will saw before him was a sad, demoralized shell of the man he had been just hours before. Will found a small place in his heart to pity the vile man.

He lifted the pistol and, without preamble, pulled the trigger.

Ten minutes later, after a final goodbye belly rub for Zanzibar, Will walked down the ramp on the other side. He stopped and pulled a large rough-cut diamond from his pocket, smoothed his note out on the machine and used the stone as a paperweight to keep it there. He hoped if it was ever discovered that they would heed his warning. This machine was dangerous, especially if Andres had been right about being able to go to other places as well. From a military security standpoint, the machine was simply an unacceptable risk. Will feared how his government might abuse it as much as he did others. Yes, it is better to simply shut the thing down.

Steadfast in the decision, Will walked down and climbed onto the floating raft to begin his final extradition from the cavern. When he reached the other side he said, "It's done. Let's get this place blown."

CHAPTER FIFTEEN

May 8ᵗʰ, 2019

Nausea swept over him even more strongly than the spray coming off the bow of the fishing trawler. They weren't fishing today. The throttle was wide open as the thirty-year-old vessel pushed its limits to the redline. Their passenger was paying more than enough for a whole new boat, much less just a new engine. And he was in a hurry. Rushing toward a stolen destiny.

For six months, he had lived in exile on the island and off the radar of the U.S. Authorities. His accommodations on the small South Pacific island would have seemed like a vacation paradise for most travelers, but to Gavin David it had been a prison, keeping him from fulfilling his destiny. The untimely fire in Genna had inadvertently unearthed his search for Cibola. The residents, and even his own workforce, thought he was greedily searching for gold beneath the ridge upon which Genna had been built. No, he was much more ambitious than that. His search for one of the fabled Seven Cities of Gold was not based on greed, at least not in the traditional sense. He was the rightful heir to a vast kingdom of riches that had been ruled by his great-great-great grandfather, Andres David.

It had been nearly twenty years since Gavin had discovered the safe deposit boxes, stuffed with uncut diamonds and a journal. The journal told a very unusual story, one that Gavin believed wholeheartedly.

Unfortunately, the entrance to the kingdom itself was described somewhat vaguely, and since even before his ancestor's time it had become wrapped in legends and myths about the Seven Cities. He knew much of the truth, but still had many questions that needed to be answered.

Gavin had been chasing leads about gold deposits around Idaho for a number of years. He knew that he was closer than he had ever been. He had been certain that the upper Salmon River region was the location. Rumors of a large gold deposit under Genna were well enough established that he had pledged to invest fifteen-million dollars in an infrastructure project that gave his team access and rights to whatever was beneath the ridge. It didn't work out the way that he had hoped. Some nosey political consultant had stumbled upon the operation at an inopportune moment. That had directly led to his exile. But he would pay. James Augustine was on his short-list of retribution.

Luckily, he had built a great network of people that would feed him new leads. This waypoint stone marker that had been discovered was remarkable, if it turned out to be authentic. The translator had sent him pictures. The second he had seen them; he had rushed to arrange transport back to the continental U.S. This fishing trawler would take him to coastal Oregon where he would arrive without government scrutiny and make his way to the Boise area in nearby Idaho.

His encrypted satellite phone chirped. He stepped into the cabin before answering. "Yes."

"Sir, I have followed them most of the way to the site."

"Most of the way?"

"They went off-road, into terrain that I couldn't follow. But I am sending the drone up now. I'll find them. It's just two academics, once I find them there will be no problem, rest assured."

"I never rest. Have you identified the second person? What have you discovered about Dr. Angeline?"

"No sir. No ID on the second target. He doesn't appear to be from the Professor's department, but that's all we know thus far. As for the Professor, well, he too seems cloaked in secrecy. He is very well-funded from some unconventional governmental sources. He was a scholar of some note until about two years ago, then he seemed to drop off the map, academically. Nobody seems to know what happened to cause the change."

"Send me the coordinates of the spot that they went off-road. Also, send me a copy of the drone footage."

"Yes, Sir."

"I will be on the ground tomorrow morning. Find them."

"Yes, Sir."

Gavin disconnected the call and rushed back up to the deck and hurled over the starboard rail. His system should be more than empty by now, but he was still feeling green. He wiped his mouth before shouting up to the Captain, "More speed!"

He needed to get off this damn boat, it is difficult to act royal whilst puking your guts up. But royal he was.

CHAPTER SIXTEEN

May 8th, 2019

The halogen lights gave the entire cavern a totally different look. The light beams seemed to be absorbed by the strange metal and then it was served back to the room as an amber glow. The effect was magical. The dark cavern, with some strange metal in it, transformed into a shining pyramid, reflecting and casting shadows into just the dark remote corners.

"I am still amazed at how clean the metal stayed. It's almost as if there is some negative ionic energy that repels dirt and dust." James gawked.

"The metal is definitely unlike anything that I

have ever seen. Which begs the question: Who built it? And when?"

They wandered the upper ledge, by the machinery, but the light truly revealed nothing that they hadn't seen with the flashlights. There were no writings, no markings, not even any suggestion that people had been here besides the note that William Clark had left. Stuart, picked up the paperweight that had held the note in place for more than two-hundred years. It was about the size of a child's fist, slightly cylindrical in shape and a frosted opaque texture. He held it up to one of the halogen lights.

"James, do you know what this is? I think it's a diamond! It's huge, too. This one stone could have set Clark up, financially, for life but he chose to leave it behind as a paperweight. Why? Where did it come from?"

"That's a diamond?"

"I am pretty sure that it is."

"That's huge!"

Seeing nothing to really investigate, James wandered over to the rock pile to see if there was anything of interest, or if it was just scrap. He rolled a few rocks out of the way and saw that what he thought were scraps of the strange metal alloy were actually connected. He tugged it out of the debris pile.

"Check this out, I think it was a chair of some sort. It's all bent up now, but..."

"Well, that's more than we've found anywhere else here. At least we can take a sample of it to the lab and get it tested. This is quite frustrating. Here we have what should be the find of the century, and yet there is nothing to go on. Nothing to investigate. We have a pyramid and the machinery, but no other signs of life aside from the note and now that chair. I am embarrassed to admit that I don't know what to do here. No paintings, carvings, papers, no symbols... there is nothing here that helps us put the pieces together."

James was absentmindedly fiddling with the chair when it suddenly sprung back into shape. He jumped back and watched as the legs popped back into the proper angles and even the dents repaired themselves. Within just a few seconds the throne was completely smooth, shiny and sturdy.

"Whoa! Did you see that?"

"It's like a spring steel or something. It's malleable, yet remembers what it is supposed to be. Fascinating."

"And this whole place seems to be made of the same stuff."

"But what is it. What's its purpose?" Stuart asked rhetorically.

"Given the lack of artifacts here, maybe we

should focus on figuring out what the machine is. Let's try to power it up." James said.

"I suppose that if we figure out what the machine does, that will give us more clues as to who built it."

"Of course, Clark's note seemed to be a warning against just that."

"William Clark's note tells us two things: First, it tells us that this thing was operational then, just some two-hundred-fourteen years ago. That's good, it is likely that we can get it going again. The second thing is that whatever he saw, he couldn't explain. People then were very superstitious, and things that were unexplainable, generally, ended up being attributed to God, if they were good, or demons, if they were bad. Especially, by uneducated people. Remember Clark was always embarrassed about his lack of an education. His understanding of whatever bothered him would have naturally found the most common explanation at the time, Gods and demons. I don't place too much faith in that particular assessment."

The two men scoured the machinery looking for anything resembling a switch or button, some way to turn the thing on. After about ten minutes, they realized that there simply were no controls on the thing anywhere.

"What now?" James asked.

"Honestly, I have no idea."

The two stood there frustrated and staring at the mechanism. Realization hit James.

"Professor, you were wrong." He paused getting his thoughts together, "Clark's letter told us three things. The line about Gods and demons. There was more to it."

The river opens the doorway to gods and daemons alike.

"The river is the power source! Those turbines that we saw down there. The waterflow drives them to create power. It doesn't need a switch, as long as water flows the machine has power."

They both rushed to the stairs and down into the riverbed, the turbines were in the shadows at the far end of the cavern. James grabbed one of the halogen light stands as they ran by, so they could in-spect the turbines. There were nine uniquely shaped cylinders with razor-sharp curved vanes wrapped around the circumference, all made of the same mysterious metal as everything else. Though they couldn't see and cables or wires connecting the tur-bines and the machinery up on the ledge, it was ob-vious that their purpose was to power the facility.

James started at the far turbine and gave it a spin to ensure that it still spun properly. As it did so, the metal in the facility began to glow slightly. Noticing a slight change, James moved down and spun two then three at a time and the glowing became more apparent.

"Let's go figure out how to get the water flowing."

The two loaded most of their necessary equipment up onto the ledge by the machines, then drove what was left out of the cavern with the Range Rover. Upon exiting the tunnel, Stuart spun the wheel sharply and drove up the steep embankment and onto the path, nearest the cavern entrance. Stuart dug around through the boxes for a moment, filling his pockets as he did so, then he turned and said, "Let's go for a walk."

The two rambled through the rock dry riverbed, careful to be on the lookout for loose rocks and sinkholes as they made their way toward the Salmon river. As they approached the levy, it became obvious how Lewis and Clark had managed to divert the tributary from flowing off of the main trunk of the river. The cliffside had a sheared off face and dropped the rock right across the river. Over the years, sand, silt, and sediment from the other side had created a mortar-like sealant that bound the rocks into a veritable wall. The surface of the Salmon was only about a foot below the top of the levy.

"So how are we going to pull this off?" James asked.

"Since the water is so high, we really only need to free up the top layer or two of rock, after that the river will finish it off... I hope."

"How are we going to even break free the top layers, without getting ourselves washed down river?"

Stuart just smiled. "Oh, I have a plan."

CHAPTER SEVENTEEN

August 26th, 1805

Sweat poured off his face and down his neck, despite the coolness of the morning hour. His Indian helpers had not made nearly as much progress drilling holes as he had hoped while Will made his visit to the jungle castle. It wasn't their fault necessarily; they weren't terribly familiar with hand tools such as these and the rock dulled the drill bits quickly. The Corporal hadn't made it back with the extra black powder until the sun was beginning to set the night before. Will and Toby had been atop the canyon wall before the sunrise putting some muscle into the boring project. They had four holes left to drill. Will hoped that they had gone deep enough to get the overhang to come apart. At any rate, the only drills that they had were a foot long. It would have to do.

Though his hands were well calloused from a lifetime of hard work, he could feel blisters developing on his palms as he gripped and rotated the D-shaped hand drill and bored into the stone. He pulled the bit out of the hole to inspect it, then rubbed the dull point along his sharpening stone to freshen it up a bit. The sharpening stone worked great for his knives, but performed a bit below par on the drill bit. It was better than nothing.

From his perch, high above the river, he could see Meriwether and one of the braves stringing ropes on the hillside above the tunnel entrance. They would need to drill several holes up there as well, though not nearly as deeply. The cool crisp air and cloudless cerulean skies allowed him to see that the taller peaks in all directions still had significant snowcaps.

When they finished drilling, Will began filling the apertures with black powder, then shoving a length of match cord into the mix before filling the top with sand and gravel, and packing it down tightly.

When he finished, he stood and stretched, being on his hands and knees on the rock for several hours had put quite a kink in his back. He ran the match cord fuses to a central point, so he could light them all together, then placed a rock over them to keep them in place.

"Hello, old friend." Toby said.

Will turned to see who he was speaking to, and saw a large bald eagle glide in for a landing fifty yards away from them. The eagle stood and stared at them turning his head back and forth between the two of them and the men working above the tunnel, as if trying to figure out what they were trying to do. After a moment, it spread its wings, one of which had a hump along the top where an old injury had healed, and dove off the edge.

"Okay, Toby. Let's go see how the Captain is doing on his part of the project."

They jumped on their horses and raced as far as they could go, until they got to the engraved boulder blocking the path.

"Go ahead and help them, I'll be there in a moment." Will said to Toby.

After, now, having made two journeys through the portal Will felt a sudden connection with those that had gone before him and felt the need to immortalize that bond on this boulder. He wanted to think of something clever, but in the end, he pulled out his hunting knife and scratched his initials into the rough stone. *W.C.*

To him, the '*C*' looked more like a jagged scar in the stone, but it was the best that he could do in the moment. He skirted around the boulder and went to see if he could help Meri with getting the charges set on Pyramid Mountain, as they had taken to calling it.

After some failures at filling the horizontal holes that had been drilled into the face of the mountain, Toby had come up with an ingenious solution. He had taken several sheets of paper from Meriwether's journal and rolled the gunpowder and a fuse into it, like a fat cigar, and folded the ends of the paper closed to seal it in. They simply slid these powder sticks into the holes and they were ready to detonate.

"If we are going to hide this thing, shouldn't we cover the inscribed stone too?" Will asked his friend.

"I wonder if powder could blow it up? I doubt it."

"We could just cover it, like we are covering the tunnel opening."

"That might work. Let's do that first, so we can have everyone upstream before we blow the other two. You never know how the river might respond to the diversion. It could very well flood this valley instead."

Toby and the other Indian went to work placing

stones around the base of the boulder and began stacking them to wall the entire stone up. Will wasn't sure why, but it looked wrong to him. Then it struck him.

"Wait, if we build a wall, it will attract attention. Why would there be a wall out here in the middle of nowhere? Those are questions that people might want to investigate, which is the last thing that we want."

He looked up at the canyon wall above the boulder. "Hey, Meri, how much powder do we have left? I am going to need a few more of those powder sticks."

Thirty minutes later they had all gathered on the path near the tunnel entrance. Will struck a match and touched it to the fuse which ran from the canyon wall to the pathway. It took nearly five minutes for the fuse to reach the explosives before the BOOM! echoed through canyon and rocks flew like shrapnel across the river, cutting down a small tree on the far side.

It was obvious from the concussion of the blast that Toby's wrapped powder sticks packed a more potent punch than gunpowder by itself. They walked around the corner to get a good look at the blast zone. It worked perfectly, the stone was smothered in rocks and debris. More importantly, it looked very much like a natural rock slide.

"Great! Now it's time for the big boom. We'll close the cave once the water has stopped running."

The four jumped on their horses and galloped back up atop the canyon. Will handed his reigns to Meriwether and walked over to where the match cord fuses had been run, leaving the others nearly one-hundred yards back from the edge.

"Ready?" Will asked, getting nods from the other three. "Fire in the hole!"

CHAPTER EIGHTEEN

May 8ᵗʰ, 2019

"Fire in the hole!" The Professor shouted with perhaps a bit too much exuberance.

He had spent the last hour putting shaped Semtex charges in the spaces between rocks along the levy, then he went back and inserted remotely-triggered detonators. He had used Semtex only one other time and he had saved what was left from that job, for a rainy day. The skies were clear, but today was that rainy day.

They had set up a video camera in the cavern so they could witness, belatedly, the awakening of the facility as the first gush of water hit the turbines.

Stuart followed his warning with a press on the detonation app on his phone, which triggered a series of explosions stronger than either he or James expected.

One of the top rocks tumbled into the dry riverbed, followed immediately by another, then physics and the power of water finished the rest as a torrent punched a hole in the center of the wall and raced down the rocky gorge filling every nook and cranny in the mad dash toward the tunnel. A three-foot wall of water crashed into the tunnel and flowed into the cavern before pushing through and spinning the nine turbines for the first time in two centuries.

The explosion, momentarily, took James back to the fire in Genna and the exploding electrical transformers and propane tanks. The mini-PTSD episode was quickly washed away as he watched the power of dihydrogen oxide, water was indeed the most powerful and adaptive force on earth. Power and grace in perfect balance.

The two men stood alongside the SUV watching the video feed, from within the cavern, on an iPad. From the camera's vantage point they could see the pyramid and its equipment power up. The strange metal began glowing and the glass screens came to life, flashing symbols and pictures of some sort. The glowing metal was mesmerizing, neither man had seen anything like that before. The spotlights and floodlights were now redundant as the entire chamber filled with a golden light.

"That's amazing."

"That looks like a city of gold, even though we know that it isn't. It is Cibola, huh?"

"It's definitely something."

"How are we going to get in now? I hadn't really thought about that. That water is flowing awfully fast, and knowing that those turbine things are at the end makes the idea of just jumping in and swimming sound like a really bad idea." James asked.

Stuart paced around the vehicle, and stared directly at the tunnel while thinking about that very question. *How do we get in and get back out? We'd never be able to swim against this current.* As he was asking himself that question, he smacked his shin on the winch sticking off the front bumper of the Range Rover. Gasping in pain and with blood dripping down onto his sock, it came to him. The winch, it was the solution. He limped to the passenger side door and dug through the glove box. It wasn't there. He flipped open the center console and moved the napkins and CD cases out of the way. There resting on the bottom, where it had been since he bought the vehicle, was the winch's remote control.

"James," he held up the remote, "the winch has a

remote, we'll be able to control both our insertion and extraction."

"Great idea... though, I don't suppose you have a wetsuit?"

"You are not that lucky." Stuart laughed.

CHAPTER NINETEEN

May 8th, 2019

"I've got them, Boss. They disappeared for a while, but the drone just found them. I thought you said these guys were archaeologists?"

"They are, why?" Gavin replied.

"Because these guys just blew up a riverbank and flooded a canyon. With Semtex no less. This doesn't seem like preserving history. It has a familiar military feeling about it."

"You're sure it was Semtex?"

Sebastian clenched his jaws shut to keep him from responding this blowhard. He hated guys like Gavin 'Da-veed'. They were born with more money than God, yet had no real-world life experiences to fall back on, so they paid guys like him to handle the hard stuff. Sebastian had to admit that his bank accounts liked Mr. David quite a bit, but personally talking to the guy sent his blood pressure up a few notches far too frequently. He unclenched his jaws and exhaled.

"Yes, Sir. I have used it and smelled it many, many times. It was Semtex."

"There are some gray areas in his file, you've seen it. Not to mention the rumors about a blown-up temple that was connected to him in some way. The government has done a good job keeping a lid on details about whatever went down. Perhaps he has a shadier history than we know. Either way, I just got into Boise. I need to make one stop to speak with the translator and then I will head your way. Figure out what they are up to A.S.A.P."

"Will do, Mr. David... I mean Da-veed. Sorry, Sir."

Gavin disconnected the call. He was on the brink of claiming his destiny, he could feel it. Unfortunately, he was also terribly frustrated by the lack of progress. They knew so much about what happened in this world, but the holes in the intelligence files of Professor Stuart Angeline left too much uncertainty for comfort. The fact that the other man working with him was a complete mystery added to the frustration. And then there was Fredrick. *Well, I will deal with Fredrick momentarily*, he thought as he pulled into a parking space at Boise State University.

It was an act of divine provenance that Fredrick stumbled into his life when he did. Fredrick had several problems in 'real' life, despite his obvious genius with languages and symbols. It may have been the arrogance that accompanied his genius that led to his gambling debts. Debts held by very violent people. Fredrick always assumed that being the smartest one at the table would pay off. And it sometimes did, in the short-term. The irony was that Fredrick never figured out why his debts kept piling up. He never realized that it wasn't the smartest one at the table that won, it was the one that owned the table that inevitably won. Gavin invested in the infrastructure of an extensive informational network. One of those investments was the acquisition of Fredrick Schmidt's debt; that investment would pay off momentarily.

His Berluti Scritti calf-leather loafers clicked on the tiled floor and echoed down the narrow hallway. When he got to the appropriate door, he didn't bother knocking instead he pushed his way into the cluttered office.

"Fredrick!"

Fredrick looked up at the tall, lean well-dressed man. He had never met him before, but the voice was one that he recognized, and it sent a chill down his spine.

"Good to finally meet you." He said, somewhat awkwardly. Truthfully, he didn't even know the man's name, but there was no doubt about who he was.

"Have you finished my translations?"

"Finished, oh my, no. Half of these are virtually dead languages. I told you it would take several days. You can't rush these or you may get a completely different message."

"And I told you that I expected them to be done when I got here. Maybe I should give you back to the Virlucci Brothers."

Fredrick's eyes went wide when he heard their name, fear based on mob stereotypes and movies is still a deep fear for the one who believes it. Gavin had no idea if they were rough and tumble guys or not. But he used the threat for a purpose, his purpose, his destiny.

"How many have you translated?"

"Fourteen, no wait... sixteen are complete, nine or ten more are partially translated."

"Send the translations to my phone, now!"

Fredrick made a few clicks on his computer keyboard as he cut & pasted it into a message. Moments later Gavin's phone dinged as they arrived.

"Fredrick, look at me. I need you to look in my eyes so that you can see that I am serious. I have a two-hour drive to make. During that time, you will finish all of the partial ones and send them to me as well, because if you don't get them to me by the time I get to my destination, I swear that I will feed you your own entrails. Do you understand me?"

Fredrick blanched, inwardly cursing Stuart Angeline for bringing this mess to him, though he was simultaneously kicking himself for getting into such a deep hole that he was now at this man's mercy. "I understand."

"Do not disappoint me." Gavin commanded as he turned to leave. It was time to go find Cibola, and his destiny.

CHAPTER TWENTY

August 27th, 1805

The dust hung in the air like a misty fog before succumbing to the pull of gravity. The three blasts over only about an hour's time had coated everyone and everything with a fine layer of dust. But their goal had been accomplished; the river was but a trickle and that trickle was diminishing by the minute, leaving little but a rocky path through the canyon.

The six men, mounted their horses and headed back to Chief Cameahwait's camp. Will had been gone from their basecamp and the rest of their party for more than three days. He was tired and, admittedly, frustrated by the outcome of their search for the City of Gold. He trotted up beside Meriwether.

"What are we going to tell the President?" He asked, low enough so the others couldn't hear.

"I think we have to tell him the truth."

"Thomas may not try to use this for nefarious purposes, but who knows who might be in charge down the road."

"It doesn't matter, we serve at the pleasure of the President. He gave us an order to find this place and report back. We may have already acted in a manner above our paygrade anyway, by blowing the place. I think he trusts us, and I think we need to trust him to make the right choices."

"He also wanted transparency in this expedition and ordered us to document and chart all of our findings. Are you suggesting that we include this in our journals?"

"Yes, today we went to the river to go fishing, but alas, a rock slide upstream caused the river to run dry, thus limiting our bounty of Salmon... or some such mundane drivel."

"Seriously?"

"Yes, write another boring daily entry. Nothing remarkable. They will blend in with all the others. Though it is likely that nobody will ever read it anyway."

The two rode in silence, save for the clips and

clops of their equine companions. They wound through the rolling hills and open meadows, all beginning to brown from the long dry summer season. Will couldn't help but reflect on the last few days and their journey.

"Who knew that this brown mountainous trail would lead us into a jungle, all in a single day?"

"Yes, that piece was quite amazing. The devil really did outdo himself by building a machine that was so mesmerizing that it could make a man believe he was a god."

"Do you really believe that? That the devil built it?"

"For now, I have to."

"Why?"

"Because it certainly wasn't built by man, if it wasn't built by the devil himself then, well, we would have to re-examine all of our beliefs about everything. I am not prepared to do that. Someday, perhaps, I will become more philosophical about it. Today, I have to believe that we are doing God's work, and shutting that place down was part of it. Besides, I still depend on God to protect us as we continue our journey. We have much more to do, in treacherous lands, before we get to the coast."

Meriwether wasn't lying, but he also wasn't willing to be forthcoming about the depth of his new doubts. What terrified him the most wasn't national security, which was ever-practical Clark's primary concern. No, it was a much deeper than that. Lewis had been described as a dreamer and an intellectual, but this facility--that blasted machine—had his mind spinning. There were really only two viable explanations, both of which brought conflict between his dreamer side and his more intellectual one. Had he not been a key aide to the President, he might write it off to a governmental project that was classified. But he had been. He had seen all the intelligence reports and communications that came across Thomas Jefferson's desk. He knew that Thomas believed this to be Cibola, the City of Gold, as rumors and expeditions for nearly three-hundred-years suggested.

Therefore, Occam's Razor suggests that there must have been some advanced civilization, prior to recorded history, that built the facility and the machine. Not only that, but they had built the machine in the African jungle as well, and if Andres was to be believed, there had to be more across the world.

Shutting this one down had solved Will's immediate security concerns, but from a global perspective Meri wondered whether they had changed anything at all. But the God-king was dead, that was probably a good thing for the world. Men of ego, in search of power, would always strive to exploit something that gives them an advantage. This ability to cross the globe in the blink of an eye would undoubtedly give them the advantage that they are seek.

"You know him better than I do. Can we trust Toby to keep quiet about this place?" Meriwether asked.

"Honestly, I think he knew more about this place than he ever let on from the beginning."

"That doesn't really answer the question, though, does it?"

"It might. He didn't tell us what he knew. Though he saved my life at least twice, so he also wasn't trying to impede our search for it. I think the three of us need to have a frank discussion about it."

"He never did go inside and see what we did, so I suppose it's only the location of it that he knows."

"I have learned not to underestimate what Toby knows."

The Captain called out to the four men riding ahead, "Corporal, take the Shoshone and ride ahead to the basecamp and let them know that we will be arriving shortly. Toby, why don't you stay back here with us?"

Toby slowed his horse and allowed Lewis and Clark to catch up to him, as the other three galloped off ahead.

"Toby, do you understand the word secret?"

He nodded in the affirmative.

"Can we count on you to keep this location secret?"

Toby considered the question, "It been secret long before white man come looking for it. I suspect it stay secret long after we are gone."

"So other Shoshone know where it is?"

Toby smiled, "Toby not special. Many know, Nez Perce too. Only a few that have been there come back. We do not glorify such things. We tell nobody. My ancestors even make scary name for it to keep people away. *River of No Return*."

"Do your ancestors know when it was built?"

"Yes. It built before time of Shoshone. It built even before Agaimpaa flow. They create river."

"Who is they?"

"Whoever build it."

"So, you don't know?"

Toby shook his head, "I guess that part secret too."

"I suppose that is best."

CHAPTER TWENTY-ONE

May 8th, 2019

Gavin David pulled off the highway and followed the directions to Sebastian's vehicle, then pulled up and parked beside it. Sebastian was sitting on the hood alternating his attention between an iPad and the drone's remote control. He wasn't an overly large man, he stood only about five-foot-eight, but his bearing was one of confidence and barely restrained aggression. As Mr. David approached, Sebastian handed him the iPad without any other acknowledgement: verbal or visual. He remained focused on piloting the drone.

"What am I looking at?"

"Hang on, I am just swinging it back around... Okay, there. See the river? That wasn't there this morning. They blew the riverbank of the Salmon river about a half mile upstream from what you are seeing here."

Gavin followed along on the iPad watching the river flow through a canyon. "How far is it from here? And what are they doing?"

"They are parked just under one Klick away, over that ridge. Since they blew the river, they have just been standing by their vehicle watching the water flow."

"Klick?"

"About half a mile, roughly. Watch the screen, the drone will be rounding the bend in about five seconds and you'll be able to see them."

Gavin watched as the drone followed the river, "There it is. Wait, where are they?"

"They were there by the Range Rover just two minutes ago. Maybe they are sitting inside it?"

"Take it down to look."

"Sir, that will draw attention."

"I don't care... I want to know where they are."

Sebastian maneuvered the drone down behind the SUV then crept it up along the right side, just above window height. Finally, it reached the passenger-side door. Gavin watched the screen intently. It was empty.

"Goddamnit! Where the hell did they go? Get some altitude and find them."

Sebastian pulled back on the control stick and the drone lifted upwards: thirty feet, fifty feet, one-hundred feet, all the way to five hundred feet. He scanned around the far section of the path. He swung back around looking for a cave or opening in the mountain. Near the top of the peak the camera showed a depression, not really a cave, that had a large nest of sticks and feathers. Clearly, this could not have been it; the two men wouldn't have been able to climb up to that point that quickly. He continued to scan the hillside suddenly the drone shook violently. He lost all control as he watched the screen on the remote. The image jerked wildly this way and that before a loud screech echoed through the canyon. Suddenly, the image barreled straight into the mountainside before going dark.

"What the hell was that?"

"Sounded like a pterodactyl. I need to go get it. That's a five-thousand-dollar drone."

"I don't care about the drone. You need to find them without getting caught. I don't want them to know we are on to them, yet."

"I'll be right back." Sebastian announced before he sprinted off up the ridge. He was still in pretty good shape, though he hadn't done any hill training since he left Afghanistan. Still, he made short work of the hill and was soon making the descent down the path on the far side. He could see the remnants of his drone lying on the hillside above the river cave. Another loud caw sounded which caused him to look up at the source. An enormous bald eagle stood in the depression near the peak, his wings spread wide; though Sebastian couldn't tell if it was a show of celebration for his victory over the drone or a warning. He looked at the majestic raptor and noticed that one wing had a large lump along the top edge where an old injury had healed.

If they only knew how old that injury was, Sebastian would have been in awe of the creature. As it was, he was pissed at it. He went to retrieve the bits of his destroyed drone. The eagle must have decided that Sebastian posed no threat, as it turned around to settle into his nest, the back side of which was built around a small pointed peak of a glowing golden metal, he laid down with its backside pressed up against the alloy point, just as it had for nearly two-hundred-twenty years.

Sebastian gathered the important pieces of the drone, then scanned the area once more looking for the two archaeologists. He saw no sign of them anywhere.

Where do they keep disappearing to?

He wandered over to investigate the Range Rover more closely. There was no sign of them whatsoever. Even their footprints ended at the river's edge. That's when he noticed it. The winch cable streamed off the front-end of the Range Rover and disappeared into the water.

He hustled back to his car, and his employer. "Boss, I know where they are!" he shouted, once he got close enough.

"You saw them?"

"Well, no. Not exactly." He gathered his words, then continued, "They are inside the mountain. They tethered themselves to the winch cable on the SUV and entered through the stone scar that the river flows into."

"Inside the mountain? Of course." He started to pace, thinking out loud. "It all makes sense. It had to be hidden." He pulled out his phone to look at the translations, but he had no signal here, no cell. "Shit. No data. I know one of the translations mentioned something about *'the water opens the gate'*. Now I understand why they blew the levy." He turned to Sebastian. "How quickly can you round up a team?"

"I have four on standby, in Boise."

"Great, let's go get them kitted up. We need some supplies; we are about to go on an adventure unlike anything you have ever seen. Plus, I need to stop and visit a friend."

"Would you like me to disable their vehicle so that they can't leave before we get back?"

"If I guess correctly, they won't be leaving anytime soon. But go ahead and make sure that they don't, we need to contain this."

CHAPTER TWENTY-TWO

May 8th, 2019

The turbulence as they traversed the tunnel was much more significant than either of them had expected, but the stiffness of the winch cable helped them remain under control. Once they crossed out of the tunnel and into the cavern, they were amazed to see that the metal itself didn't simply reflect light, but emitted an amber hue which cast the entire place with an entirely new look.

"Now I can see why the legend of a City of Gold came from."

"Yes, but notice the translations that we have all mentioned not a city of gold, but a golden city or a golden pyramid. In our greed, we--and those before us--only thought of it as a literal city of gold, but the translations have proven to be correct." Professor Angeline spun around, taking it all in. "For the first time in two-hundred-fifteen years this place is powered up and running as if no time has passed. Amazing."

"Take a look at this." James said. Standing in front of the machinery, he stared at the clear glass screen hanging at eye level. Symbols flashed intermittently, not through it digitally, like a computer or TV screen, but on it as if they had substance. They didn't switch to the next symbol, so much as morph into it.

"What kind of projection system is this? It's like a solid hologram, which makes no sense to me." The Professor stated to himself as he watched. He scanned around it, but he saw no buttons or keyboard type of controller. A lifelong student of history, Stuart had seen his fair share of symbols and markings, but only one of these looked even remotely familiar to him. That one looked very much like a Celtic Knot. It wasn't exactly the same but it was definitely derivative of it. He caught himself, *more likely the Celtic knot was derived from this symbol.*

He took out his cell phone and recorded a video of the screen flashing through its sequence of symbols. Once it completed its cycle, he stopped recording and switched to the regular camera and took still shots of each individual symbol, seventeen of them in all.

Unable to resist the urge, James reached out to touch the three-dimensional image on the screen. The Professor moved to stop him, but his reaction wasn't quite quick enough. James' fingertip touched the image which froze in place. It was solid and coarse, like stone, but similar to the strange metal that the machine and the facility were built from, it warped and then formed around his fingertip.

Suddenly, everything changed as if time froze, the images stopped flashing and the machine itself began to hum and though it didn't vibrate, the air in the chamber seemed to.

"What did you do?"

"I don't know. Clearly, I activated something." James said sheepishly.

The three-dimensional image began to flash and stood out even further from the flat screen. James opened his hand and grabbed the symbol. It was solid, and 'real'. To their right the screen on the next piece of machinery began to flash. He pulled his hand away and the heavy stone symbol came with it.

"How in the world..." the Professor's words failed him as he watched.

In his world, the world of archaeology, you simply refrained from trying to activate anything.

Usually the only mechanisms were there to keep people out of tombs or temples. Activating them could spring any number of ingenious traps devised by the ancients. But here, staring at what was likely the most ancient machine he had ever encountered, it also seemed like the most futuristic one. Though the energy had changed in the room, it didn't feel malevolent, and the fact that so many had somehow made the pilgrimage to this place and inscribed messages on the boulder outside gave him the feeling that they just might survive this machine's activation.

The screen on the other mechanism began flashing even more rapidly. Finally, the thoughts floating around the back of his mind connected. "It's a key. The key is created by this one, I bet you take it to that one. Go put it up against that screen. Wait, hold your hand out."

James held his open palm up. Stuart quickly snapped another picture of it. The two then walked a few steps to the next screen. The symbol was similar to a fleur-de-lis, but instead of three flower petals bound together, it was more jagged, like lightning bound together.

"I don't see anywhere to put it. If it's a key, shouldn't it be inserted into something?"

"I think everything we think we know about everything is about to change. Hold it up to the screen, just like how you took it from the first one."

Light from the screen seemed to reach out and grab the stone symbol from James' hand, then spun it around three times before it flexed outward, then drawn into the screen. Instantly the ramp and the two pillars on either side of it began to glow slightly, but noticeably, more intensely. The air vibrations intensified as well, as if the entire cavern was energized, and the space between the pillars began to flow like heat waves.

"So, is this the gateway to gods and demons that Clark wrote about?" James asked, suddenly worried.

"I think it might be. Maybe it hypnotizes you or causes hallucinations. There has to be some explanation besides letting gods and demons in here. I told you, people were superstitious in those days."

"What about the other translations? The ones Fredrick sent us. If we needed to take that one literally, maybe we need to re-examine the others to ensure that we aren't reading into it."

"Good point. Let me see." The Professor dug his well-worn leather-bound journal from his pack. "Here they are!"

The hieroglyphs translate roughly to:
A golden pyramid, a flash of light and a whole new world
fills my eye.

Even the gods don't know from where to here. (or possibly from whence we came)
The runic translation is:
The gilded-gates to Valhalla begin the journey of eternal life, though strange
lands cloud the way there is a path to Odin's sanctuary.

"*A golden pyramid*, well, I think we have that one." James smiled looking up toward the pyramidion tip. "*A whole new world fills my eye...* I mean this is all fascinating and all, but I wouldn't call it a whole new world."

The Professor was focused on something that he hadn't expected. "The important piece, which I am not entirely okay with, is the last line. I think Fredrick's second translation tells us everything. *Even the gods don't know from whence we came.*"

"What does that mean?"

"Do you still have your weapon?"

"Always... why?"

"We're going for a walk."

The Professor walked over to their equipment crates and dug through and found his satellite reader, the stud finder, as James had taken to calling it. He turned it on and waited for it to go through its connection cycle. After a minute, it became obvious that it wouldn't connect to the satellites through the stone of the mountain. Hoping for the best on the other side, he stuffed the transponder into his jacket pocket.

Bracing himself against the reality shift that he thought was about to occur. "Come on."

James hadn't connected the dots yet, but followed Stuart's lead as they walked up the ramp together.

A slight breeze and a flash of light... and they were gone.

CHAPTER TWENTY-THREE

May 8th, 2019

The RAV4 flew south down the highway. Gavin David cursed, from the passenger seat, once they got into a cell service zone. Still nothing from Fredrick. He had warned him quite explicitly. Now it was time to escalate things. He sent Fredrick's file to Sebastian's phone.

"I just sent a file to your phone. Have your guys go grab him, now while we are on the way. He is going to be instrumental to us completing this mission. He's an academic, a Linguistics scholar. The file has all of his details."

"They're going to want more money to do a snatch & grab in the broad daylight."

"I don't care we need him, and his translations of the stone."

"Yes, sir." Sebastian replied while pushing a button on his phone to forward the file to the head of his team, Red. Then he placed a call to coordinate the impromptu operation.

The compact SUV roared through pine-tree-lined canyons and wound along the Payette River as groups of kayakers braved the frigid waters to run the gauntlet of category three and four rapids that peppered that stretch of the river. The two men inside spoke little, both anxious to get to Boise and get back up to the Cibola site.

In just over an hour and a half they pulled into Boise. The men were waiting at the pre-arranged rendezvous point, the parking lot of a large Army surplus store on Chindon Blvd. The men were already well enough armed to handle most anything that they came across, but they needed camping gear, rappelling gear, and dry suits with snorkels and masks.

Gavin got out and ignored the rest of the men as he walked to the Suburban that he assumed held Fredrick. Through the back window he saw a deflated version of the arrogant academic. He opened the door and slid into the seat next to him.

"All that I required was for you to do what you do best. Yet now, because you failed to deliver, I am going to require much, much more. I suggest that you do better and get the job done, if you ever want to get back to your cushy life. Have I made myself clear?"

Shoulders rolled forward in a hunched over sub-missive posture, Fredrick offered, "I am trying. It's not as easy as you think it is. What more do you want me to do?"

"You are going to decipher the stone, in situ. You are going to get me the answers that I need to find my kingdom. If you do that, you will be free to go wherever you want and your debt will be considered paid in full."

Fredrick was about to question the remark about 'my kingdom' but decided that he should just keep his mouth shut. He did have one more question. "In order to do it, I'll need WiFi. Is there a cell out there?"

Gavin clenched his jaw, then opened his door and yelled to the nearest man, "Please go tell Se-bastian to see if they have a satellite-linked laptop."

He closed the door and turned back to Fredrick, "No excuses now, Fredrick. You will do what I have asked." He climbed out and slammed the door closed, his words left hanging in the air, sending a chill up Fredrick's spine. *What have I gotten myself into?*

Thirty minutes later all seven of them, in a two-car caravan were headed back up into the mountains. The road to riches, it seemed to Gavin as he daydreamed about finally, after years of searching, fulfilling his destiny. He dreamt of half-naked native girls feeding him and an army of warriors worshipping him and enforcing his will. He dreamt of being a King, as his great, great, great grandfather had. Perhaps even a god.

Having switched into Sebastian's car, Fredrick was typing furiously trying to set up the new computer, so that it would be ready to go once they got to the site. It was slower than the T1 connection that he had at his office at the University, but it would be functional. He hadn't disclosed to Gavin that he had actually completed twenty of them. He would have been afraid to lie, he had a horrible poker face, but he felt lucky that Gavin had never asked him that question directly. *The man is a lunatic. What does he mean by 'his kingdom', anyway?*

They made short work of the road back and soon the two vehicles pulled off and parked next to Gavin's rental car. The men in the Suburban unloaded and began checking their weapons and equipment. Sebastian opened a large box, pulled out a controller into which he inserted batteries, then launched his new matte black 'stealth' drone into the azure skies to recon any changes in the situation. The Range Rover and the winch cable appeared to be exactly as they had been when they left. There was no sign of the archaeologists.

"Okay, all is clear. Get kitted up and get into your dry suits."

The men packed their packs and stowed their weapons, before stepping into the dry suits which sealed tightly from their ankles to their necks, protecting them from the still frigid water temperatures and keeping their weapons dry during the swim into the cave. All six men prepared for the mission, except for Fredrick, he would stay out by the stone and get to work. Once they were ready, and with each of them carrying a pair of flippers they began the march toward the path to the tunnel.

Sebastian spoke up, "So what's to stop your boy Fredrick from emailing or messaging someone for help while we are in the cave."

Gavin hadn't considered that possibility. He assumed fear and the reward of his life would be motivation enough to keep the academic in line. He did see the logic in Sebastian's way of thinking though, *What if...?*

"Who is the least experienced amongst your crew?"

"That would be Jones. He's good, but he's also young and dumb."

"Okay, we'll leave him to babysit the Linguist. The five of us should be able to handle anything we face on the other side."

Sebastian bit his tongue so hard that it was probably bleeding in an effort to not chastise his benefactor for suggesting that he, himself, was just one of the boys that could get things handled. The smug arrogance of a yuppie silver-spooner trying to fit in with Sebastian's seasoned vets, just because he was dressed like one of them.

"Sir, do you have any combat experience?" His mouth said in direct contradiction to what his brain was telling it to do.

"I have led a number of operations. Not in combat, but in my line of work, things get messy from time to time."

"My guys are professional soldiers, let us do the handling of things. You can swoop in at the end and take all the glory. And please try not to shoot me or any of my guys with that thing, this isn't a shooting range. Hell, we don't even know what we are up against. Only well-trained soldiers can adapt to situations that arise in the field without getting someone killed. Please let us do what you pay us for."

As they came over the rise, Sebastian pulled his Magpul FMG-9 folding submachine gun from inside the zipper of his dry suit and took point position as he unfolded the rare weapon. The FMG-9 packed quite a punch, yet folded to the size of a laptop battery for concealed carry. That feature also made it ideal for stuffing it into a dry suit. As the point person, he ensured that the area was clear of hostiles before the rest of the team reached the Range Rover and the river's edge. There was no sign of the two archaeologists.

"Jones, strip off your dry suit and stay here to look after Mr. Schmidt. He is not to communicate with anyone on that laptop, only look at research. Is that understood?"

His face deflated some at missing out on the action, but his dutiful reply was simply, "Yes, Sir."

Gavin and Jones escorted Fredrick over to the inscribed boulder. Gavin whipped out a small, folding camp table for him to set the laptop on. He promptly took the laptop from Fredrick and placed it on the table.

"Are we clear on what I expect from you?"

The question elicited nothing but a nod from the Linguist who was lost in the sea of symbols adorning the boulder. Seeing that Fredrick was properly motivated by the etchings, Gavin turned his attention to Jones. "You are to be in a position to see his computer screen at all times, do you understand?"

"Yes, Sir."

"Good. If he tries anything shoot him. There are other linguistic experts that we can bring in if need be." He stated loud enough to ensure that Fredrick could hear through the symbolic fog that he was in. He turned and rejoined the other men who were ready to infiltrate the facility.

Sebastian spoke to the team. "Davis, Garcia and myself will drop in first and secure the site. Donny, you give us forty-five seconds then bring up the rear after helping ensure Mr. Dav-eed gets properly hooked to the cable. Clear?"

With that Sebastian and the lead team slid their flippers on and slid their masks into place before clipping the carabiners from their lead lines to the winch cable. They stepped into the chilly water and one-by-one leaned back and let the current take them away. Though there were a few bumps on the backside from submerged rocks, they raced mostly unscathed through the tunnel and into the surprisingly well-lit cavern. They came to a sudden stop as their carabiners hit the winch hook's clamp at the end of the cable. Sebastian, being the first in line, brought his face above the surface and scanned for any activity. He saw no activity on the lower level and unhooked from the line. With the aid of his flippers he smoothly and quietly made his way to the elevated rock platform. Once he climbed onto it he pulled the FMG-9 back out and pointed it at the upper ledge to provide cover for the other two.

Garcia unhooked next and the former Navy SEAL deftly swam around the platform and reached the stairs at the far side. He too pulled his weapon from his suit and aimed it up the stairs before waving Davis over.

Davis unclipped his carabiner from the cable, but the current caused him to drift to the other side of the line. As he swam under to clear it the winch hook caught on the back of his dry-suit. The snag upset his balance and caused his feet to swing wide into the main current. He fought to free himself and kicked vigorously to maintain his position. He felt the material of his dry-suit rip, but still he didn't come free. Panic began to set in, and he knew he was making too much noise, but he was hooked like a salmon on a trolling rig.

Without warning his suit ripped further and the hook broke free as he was pulled into the main current. He paddled and kicked furiously as he was swept downstream, no longer concerned with the noise level, he yelled, "Sebasti..."

The scream was cut short as he was sucked into the turbines. The lights flickered briefly as Davis' body was pulverized by the rapidly spinning and razor-sharp turbine blades. In seconds, Davis was gone and the lighting returned to normal.

Sebastian bowed his head sullenly. "Damnit!" he said under his breath. Davis was a good man, and a good soldier. They had served together for two tours in Afghanistan and several private security gigs since then. It hurt, but he had a mission to complete.

He signaled to Garcia, pointing to his eyes, then to the top of the ledge. Garcia sprinted silently to the top of the stairs and laid the muzzle of his rifle on the top step, scanning the ledge through his scope.

"All clear, boss."

Clear? Sebastian thought, *where the hell are the archaeologists?*

He was shaken from his thoughts as a blur splashed through the water and slammed to a stop at the hook clamp. *Gavin!*

He leapt into the water and swam to the line to make sure that they lost nobody else on his watch, especially not their client. He unhooked Gavin's clip and purposefully drug him over to the calmer waters near the platform before releasing him. Donny's clip had just snapped to a halt on the line and Sebastian raced out to help him get safely ashore.

Once Gavin and Donny were both atop the platform, Sebastian pulled himself out and rolled flat on his back. He was exhausted, but he knew that what he felt was more from the emotional toll of losing Davis than it was from the physical exertion.

The emotional loss he could deal with later, after this was all over. The fact that his small team was down to three was a harder pill to swallow. He still had a mission to complete, he wondered if the three of them: Donny, Garcia, and himself were up to the task. Despite the pretenses, Gavin was the client, not a part of his team. He rolled over an onto his feet.

"Let's go find those damned Archaeologists."

CHAPTER TWENTY-FOUR

May 8th, 2019

A puff of air and a flash of light was the only indication that anything had changed. James and Stuart walked down the ramp into the cavern, similar, but definitely not identical to the one they had just been in. They were met my silence and warmth, neither of which could have been said thirty seconds before. The silence came from the lack of a rushing river, of water at least. They soon realized that the warmth was generated from a large oval fissure in the cave floor which contained a swirling and bubbling pool of molten lava.

Aside from those differences, the pyramid

looked nearly identical, as did the equipment. The golden glow had a slightly redder hue to it, likely due to the light emitted from the lava itself being added to the mix.

"How did we get here?" James queried.

"The question is: where is here?"

Stuart pulled the satellite transponder from his jacket pocket and, once again, tried to activate the connection sequence. Again, it failed to connect.

"Let's find a way out of here and figure out where we are."

"I'm not even ready to question what the hell just happened. This is like some Star Trek beaming up kind of voodoo." James said as he struggled to wrap his head around their situation.

"Especially, since this place, or I should say these places, are so ancient. Yet, the technology seems so futuristic. And it's apparently very adaptable technology. Ours was powered by water flow, and-though I have no idea how-I would bet that this one is powered by geothermal energy."

James walked around the edge of the lava pool fascinated by the way it moved and shifted. When he reached the far side, he felt a slight cool breeze on the nape of his neck as if something was breathing on him. He spun around quickly, fearing some creature had snuck up on him. But there was nothing there. The breeze continued though, now blowing on his face. He followed the direction of the breeze.

"Professor, I think there is an opening over here."

Stuart made his way over to James just as they reached the wall. James held his hand out ahead of him, feeling for the breeze as he approached a solid rock wall. When he was about a foot from the wall, he was able to see an angled crevice which opened sideways. It was all but invisible looking at it straight on, but from the right angle the opening looked wide enough to just get his shoulders through.

"Here, come on." James called as he led the way through the maze-like corridor.

The light from the metals and the lava didn't penetrate very far into the crevice and after only a dozen steps it became pitch black. He pulled a mini-Maglite from his pocket to light the way forward. With each step, the temperature dropped a few degrees. Finally, he rounded the final bend and bright sunlight and a cold wind greeted him forcefully. It took a moment for his eyes to adjust, but when they did it brought a sense of awe and amazement, coupled with a distinct fear that everything that he had ever believed about the world was false.

Stuart joined him at the mouth of the cave on a narrow ledge overlooking a massive mountain range, covered in snow. They occupied, apparently, the tallest peak of the range, as they looked down upon several peaks that were colossal in their own right. The sky was painted in the indigo, ginger, scarlet, and burnt sienna palette of a morning sunrise, broken by only a few puffy light clouds that seemed to hang at their eye-level.

"Can you get that thing to connect to the satellites now?"

"Hang on, it's trying to connect." He waiting watching anxiously. "It looks like it's having trouble triangulating the exact location." He looked at the mountain behind them, "the third satellite is likely being blocked by this peak. So, I can't get an exact location, but this says that we are somewhere on the Tibetan plateau."

"Tibet?"

"Yeah, and we better get back home before nightfall, the temperatures up here overnight will be brutally cold, even by Idaho standards."

Off to their right was a narrow stone path which ran a few dozen yards along the mountain's face before dropping off into a long set of narrow, steep steps carved directly into the mountainside. To their left, the ledge ended in an abrupt plunge down the sheer mountainside.

"Well, I guess we have two choices. We can go back home now that we know where it goes or we

can go explore a bit first and try to find out why."
James said, passively suggesting that he wanted to
look around a little bit. It's not every day that you
get to go to Tibet, after all.

"Okay, let's go take a look. But make sure your
firearm is ready, we have no idea what we might face
up here."

James nodded, and deftly drew the Smith &
Wesson Shield 9mm from the holster inside his
waistband. He ejected the magazine and inspected it
to ensure that it was loaded with the full eight
rounds, then pulled the slide back to verify one was
in the chamber before reinserting the magazine into
the pistol grip with a distinct click as it was rammed
home. Nine rounds were all he had. His extra maga-
zines were in his pack, back in the Range Rover. It
would have to do. He had always claimed that if you
were ever in a situation where you needed more
than eight shots from a compact handgun, well, you
were in deep yogurt anyway. With the uncertainty
that they were facing at the moment, he wasn't
feeling as confident as he had always preached. Of
course, he couldn't tell Stuart that.

"We're good. Let's go see Tibet." He proclaimed.

The steps were steep and narrow, treacherous by
any definition. The two made slow progress down
the mountain. After some time, the stairs came to
an end and they came to a landing at the head of a

wood-planked rope bridge which spanned a wide fissure between two separate ribs of the mountain. It swayed gently in the breeze.

James looked over the edge and instinctively stepped back when he saw that the chasm looked to fall more than five-hundred-feet down. He gazed across the span and saw that the bridge terminated at a well-manicured path that led to the entrance to some sort of building.

"The path from the cavern leads only one way, into that building. Maybe we can get some answers there." The Professor said.

"Yeah, assuming we survive the bridge crossing."

"What? The hero of the BonnFire in Genna is afraid of a measly little bridge? I think you'll survive. And to prove it, I am going to let you go first." Stuart quipped with a laugh.

"Great, I can't wait."

James wasn't really scared, though the way the narrow bridge swayed in the wind was a tad unnerving, he had faith that everything would work out exactly as it was supposed to—whether he liked it or not. In his mind, if they had taken the equivalent of a magic carpet ride to Tibet, there must be a reason for it. If God wanted him dead, there had been plenty of opportunities back in Idaho; there would be no reason for him to end up here. There had to be a purpose for his journey, and he hoped that the purpose was inside that building. Either way, he knew it would all work out. This was the mindset that he had acquired over six years of conscious contact with his higher power that he had developed and learned via his years in sobriety and in the rooms of Alcoholics Anonymous.

That mindset led to the confidence in his first step upon the blackened, aged wood of the bridge. He walked slowly but steadily across, taking in the majesty of the scenery around him, barely suppressing the urge to pull his phone out and take pictures. Despite his confidence, both hands remained on the rope rails as he made his way across the span. Suddenly he felt a new vertical movement under his feet. He looked back and Stuart was strolling across without a care in the world. Each step causing the rest of the bridge to lurch upward slightly, compounding the various movements that James was beginning to feel even more strongly as he reached the center of the span.

"Take it easy, Professor. This thing is really moving out here."

"Oh, you'll be fine. Just don't stop, one never knows how long these planks have been here. Don't want all your weight on any one of them for very long, or…"

Suddenly, with the age of the planks rattling around his cranium, James became hyper-aware of every creak and crack that the boards gave of as he moved over them, along with the increased sway caused by the movement of the two men. As smoothly and quickly as he could manage, James reached the end and was followed shortly by the Professor. James gave a quick prayer of thanks before resuming their trek.

As they crossed from the rocky bridgehead onto the manicured pathway they were amazed at the meticulous care, planning, and maintenance that had gone into what they saw. Though it was wintery weather, the flowers and plants bloomed in a kaleidoscope of colors. Ornamental trees with a multitude of colored leaves were placed perfectly in an esthetic balance in which neither the tree nor the plants dominated the space, instead they all complemented each other seamlessly. They were all one despite their individual nature. Even in the face of the blustery, breezy conditions, not a single leaf or flower petal littered the grounds.

"If this path only goes one place, why do you think they are so meticulous in their groundskeeping?" James asked.

Stuart looked around. The building ahead was cloaked by a wall so it was difficult to know exactly what it was. But he had a guess.

"I think this is either a temple or a monastery of

some sort, and their adherents keep it maintained for an occasion like this."

"But how many visitors could they possibly get?"

"Their devotion is to keeping it ready. Whether anybody comes or not, is irrelevant. Of course, I could be wrong."

They continued toward the opening in the wall, staying carefully on the path. The last thing James wanted was to disturb the peace and balance that they had constructed.

Entering through the arched doorway, they stepped into a private garden of substantial size and more ornate and splendid than anything either of them had ever seen. Though it was open-roofed, the courtyard seemed to be untouched by the wintery conditions outside the walls. Blooms and vines, shrubs and bushes encircled a majestic tree, larger than the largest of the mighty oaks, at the very center of it all, golden globes of an unidentifiable fruit weighed the mature branches down. Small statues of many deities were scattered throughout, not just Asian gods, but there seemed to be depictions of all of the gods, of all of the cultures through all eras.

The sun brought warmth to the space and a small stream fed a small waterfall on one side. It seemed that all of nature's beauty was represented in the space. Despite the wild, natural feel, keen observation showed that the garden was maintained with the same eye to detail as the path that led to it; not a leaf out of place, nor drooping flower bud to be seen anywhere. Both of them were left speechless.

They wandered the path which wound toward the great tree with the golden fruit. When they came around the final bend, both stopped abruptly. Sitting at the base of the wide white-barked trunk was a lone man dressed in the crimson pulu shemdap skirt and golden chŌgu and maroon dagang, trimmed in silk, of a high-level monk. He made no move when they approached. His eyes remained closed, his breathing even, and his body still. When he did finally react to the disturbance of his peaceful moment and open his eyes, they saw no indication of surprise or fear. No tension whatsoever.

"I have waited for you to arrive. Welcome to Adin." He said, in only slightly accented English.

"You speak English?" The Professor said.

"I speak every language," He tilted his head slightly before adding, "some better than others."

"What do you mean you were waiting for us? We didn't even know we were coming here." James asked.

"And yet, here you are."

"Excuse my colleague. Allow us to introduce ourselves. I am Professor Stuart Angeline. This is my colleague, James Augustine."

"I have awaited your arrival. Please sit." He waved his hand toward two narrow benches that blended in with the landscape so well that they hadn't even noticed them.

The monk's words and tone were even and comforting, if a bit cryptic. They took their seats and waited for him to speak. Eventually, James' impatience won the battle and he broke the ice.

"What is this place? A temple?"

"It is Adin. It is a garden, nothing more, nothing less."

"What is your role here?"

"I am awaiting your arrival."

"I don't mean today; I mean what is your title. Why is the garden here? Why is it winter outside the walls, but Spring in here? How did you know we were coming?"

"I am Adon, the servant of Adin. The garden is here, because it is here. Where else would it be? Spring is the season of new life; all life begins in Adin. I knew you were coming, where else would you go? There is only one path, it leads from Adin out into the world. But not all who come are ready."

The Professor interjected, "Ready for what, Adon?"

"Answers."

"To what?"

"To everything. You are ready, but a dark cloud

follows you and you don't even know it. You must confront the darkness from your past in order to move into your new role."

"I am thinking that you have us confused with someone else. What new role? What darkness?" James blurted out.

"No, you have been chosen. There is no mistake, otherwise you would not be here ready to start your journey."

"What role? What journey?" Stuart inquired.

"You are now Travelers."

"Of course, we're travelers. We woke up in Idaho, and now we're in a garden in Tibet!" James' exasperation showing.

"Professor, what do you study?"

"Mostly Biblical archaeology, until recently."

"Good, good. Then you will understand. How many cultures have a flood story similar to Noah's?"

"Quite a few. Gilgamesh comes to mind, but I know lots of cultures have a similar story."

"And what is unique about Quetzalcoati, or Viracocha? I realize that they aren't necessarily biblical characters, but I suspect you know what I am getting at."

"The deities of most religions and cultures tend to look like the believers. Quetzalcoati and Viracocha were unique in that they were bearded white men, worshiped by dark-skinned, nearly hairless

Mayans, Toltecs and other native 'Indian' tribes." He emphasized the last bit by making finger quotes in the air.

"Very good. Very good. Anything else?"

"Not that I can think of, off the top of my head."

"Hmm, interesting. Let me ask you this. How much sea travel did the ancients do?"

"Island to island, perhaps. Certainly, not across oceans. Until maybe the Vikings."

"So, if that is the case, how do all of the cultures have such similar stories? How did pyramids develop in both Egypt and South America if there was no trans-oceanic exploration? How did a lone white man get to South America? Unless you believe he was Quetzalcoati and Viracocha really were gods. They were the same person by the way."

"Who was the same person?"

"Quetzalcoati, Viracocha, and of course, Jesus Christ. I really thought you might have made that connection. But alas, this is all new to you. Anyway, they all had similar stories and similar technological advances because of the Travelers. There have been fifty-two of them throughout the untold history of this planet. Travelers are called to teach, inspire, and help humanity continue its progression... and occasionally to give humanity the kick in the back-side that gets it back on track. Most have statues here in the Garden of Adin to commemorate their efforts to help humanity."

"But these are all gods?"

"No, but many of them are, or were, worshiped as gods. This is something that many of them resisted, a few were smitten by the worship, but most tried to play that piece down. People think Poseidon and Neptune were different names of the same god of the sea; one Greek, one Roman. And as with most myths and legends, there is some truth and some fantasy. He was a Traveler who ventured forth from the sea and taught mankind how to sail and how to fish so that they would be self-sufficient. But what if I told you that he never actually went to Greece or Rome? Quick Professor, who is the earliest culture that you can think of that is talked about as being dominant on the seas?"

"The Phoenicians?"

"Very good, why were they dominant? Because he taught them first. He let them teach the other cultures in the area. His real name was Odon though he became known as Phodon by the Phoenicians, perhaps as a way to claim him as their own. And well, various translations led to the other three names."

"Other three? Phodon, Poseidon, and Neptune. The word 'other' implies another."

"Far away from the European and Mediterranean

cultures, he was also known by another great sea-faring people as, Odin."

"Wait, you're saying that Odin, Poseidon, Neptune, Jesus, and Quetzalcoati were all Travelers? And now you claim we are? I'm just some schmuck who found a fancy rock while out hiking and happened to live next door to a guy that could take the discovery to the next level. I'm not godly, hell, I don't even go to church."

"And yet, here you are. All of the Travelers have started by sitting exactly where you are, and most were as bewildered as you are. As I said before, all life starts in Adin, so too does all knowledge."

Adon glanced briefly away from them, looking slightly frustrated, before quickly regaining his composure. He looked directly at James, "At any rate, before we discuss any more about that, as I said, you must face the black clouds in your past. And now is the time to do it."

"Why, now?"

"Because they are coming down the path as we speak."

CHAPTER TWENTY-FIVE

May 8th, 2019

Though he knew what to expect of the portal from reading King Andres' journals, experiencing it was something completely different. The rest of his party had no idea what to expect and they were a bit flustered to say the least. Gavin eagerly searched for the exit to the cavern that they found themselves in. Luckily, the archaeologists had left footprints in the dust, around the lava pool and into the hidden, narrow crevice.

Gavin could barely contain himself. Finally, his persistence had paid off and the time to fulfill his destiny had come. He turned to the three remaining team members, before they went through the crevice.

"Okay, men. This is it. This is what we have been searching for. There were warriors guarding this facility two hundred years ago, I don't know if they have taken it upon themselves to continue guarding it in the years since the King died. But we should be prepared, just in case. These savages don't know any better, they may still be raising their sons to perform this duty. So, look sharp. And I want the two archaeologists alive... at least for now. I need to find out what else they know. Understood? My jungle kingdom awaits our return. Let's go."

Mr. David led the way, winding his way through the narrow fissure, he was surprised at the coolness of the breeze coming at him. Finally, light shone at the end of the passage and he stepped out into the daylight. *What the fuck? Where the hell is my jungle? My kingdom?*

The rest of the party stepped out and looked over the snow-covered mountainous plateau. After a heartbeat, Garcia quipped, "I have been in a few jungles in my days, but I have never seen one that looked like this. " Donny laughed.

Sebastian corrected them with a single word, "Enough!"

He knew that their already volatile and somewhat zealous benefactor would not likely react to this turn of events well.

Gavin David, for his part, made his best effort to remain composed, uttering only a single sentence quietly and calmly through grinding teeth. "Find them, whatever it takes; even if we have to melt the entire fucking glacier down."

Sebastian quickly assessed the terrain. "Well, there is only one way that they could have gone. Let's go get 'em!"

They set off down the path, and then the stone steps before coming to the bridge. Donny began to curse. The guy was fierce and fearless. Great to have at your side during battle or on a mission. His one weakness, that Sebastian had seen, was a near-crippling fear of heights. For some reason, skydiving he was fine with, but when he was supposed to have something under him--like a plank bridge—it messed with his psyche in a major way.

"You got this, Donny?" He coaxed.

"Yes, goddamnit, I've got this." He was clearly embarrassed by his affliction and that was expressed via defensiveness.

"I'll lead you get right on my tail and stare at the back of my shirt."

"Your ass isn't nice enough to keep his attention, Bas." Garcia joked.

"This is game-time Garcia, cut the crap."

"Yes, Sir."

"You will follow Mr. David, and ensure that he remains unscathed, do you understand?" Garcia nodded in the affirmative.

"Okay. Let's move."

The first two, Sebastian and Donny, stepped out onto the bridge and began to walk lightly but steadily. Donny put a hand on the back of Sebastian's vest and stared at the back of his head, as he matched his pace step for step. Once they were about one-third of the way across Gavin and Garcia began their crossing. The motion changed, but nobody seemed to be affected by it. At the halfway point, Sebastian swung M-4, that was dangling from its sling, up into ready position. He didn't believe that the two academics were a threat, but so far on this journey little had gone as planned. It never hurt to be cautious.

Sebastian felt a tug on the back of his vest which was immediately followed by the scream of a little girl. He whipped around and just caught the shoulder straps of Donny's vest as he was falling through wooden plank that had disintegrated under his boot. Donny's masculine nature was instantly replaced by the fear of a six-year-old girl as he shrieked repeatedly.

"Easy, Donny. I've got you."

Realizing that Sebastian was telling the truth,

Donny pulled his right leg back through the hole and fell to his knees, hands squeezing the ropes on either side so tightly that his knuckles turned white. His rapid shallow breathing told Sebastian that this wasn't a small phobia, but a re-enforcement of his already incapacitating fear.

"Take a deep breath and let me help you up."

"No, just go."

Sebastian turned back around and walked more purposefully toward the terminus. Once he reached the landing he turned and saw Donny crawling the last five yards on his hands and knees, one hand always clamping on the rope as he did so. Once he finally reached land, Donny rolled over on his back just grateful that he was alive.

Gavin and Garcia followed shortly thereafter and immediately spread out, weapons ready, to cover the path ahead. Sebastian tried to rally Donny and get him moving. He reluctantly got up and got into formation.

"Move out. " Sebastian ordered, and the four moved cautiously down the path toward the arched doorway in the wall and the courtyard that could be glimpsed beyond it. As they came around a turn and had a different angle view of the courtyard, he could see the two archaeologists speaking to someone dressed like a monk.

The monk's eyes connected with Sebastian's

eyes, though it felt more like he was looking through him than at them.

The monk reached his hand out and twisted it slightly, and everything changed.

CHAPTER TWENTY-SIX

Adon made eye contact with the leader of the force. He sensed conflict within him, more than malice, but as he glanced to the well-heeled man next to him, he saw everything that he needed to see.

Adon raised his right hand toward the archway and made a twisting motion. Instantly, the wall surrounding the garden began to shift, closing off that entryway and opening a new doorway on the other side.

"I will hold them off here. You two go out that way," He said, pointing at the new opening. "Get back through the gilded gates and once you do, face your past and deal with that which you have avoided dealing with. Each of you have your own battle with your demons. When you return here, then you will be ready to begin your next journey."

With that he reached into a fold in his robe and drew a long flaming sword as he leapt to his feet. "Go now!", he shouted as he moved rapidly over to where the original archway had been. James and Stuart didn't argue, they sprinted for the newly opened door.

As soon as the two stepped through, the wall shifted again closing the door to the Garden of Adin behind them. Stuart glanced back as it closed. Silently praying that they would be able to get back here. Such an amazing place and the lessons that he could learn from Adon seemed limitless.

They ran full tilt on the new path that had morphed into existence for them, leading directly toward the bridgehead. As they got near the bridge, they could see flashes of blue light and hear rapid gunshots. At the landing they could watch the battle as four men faced off against the lone figure of Adon and his sword who was more than holding his own as he stood in the archway. Standing there, behind the other three and several inches taller, James saw a face that he recognized. *What the hell is Gavin David doing here?*

Gavin David had been the mastermind behind the efforts to mine gold beneath Genna, that James had stumbled upon in the wake of the fire. Though he had never actually met the man, James had been captured and held prisoner by the people that worked for Mr. David. Gavin David's private jet had 'disappeared' from radar over the Pacific Ocean in the aftermath of the scheme's crumble. He had seen his picture many times during the ensuing investigation. There was no doubt in his mind that that was who it was. He instinctively started to move back toward the fray.

Stuart grabbed his arm. "He's stalling until we get to safety. Let's go."

"That guy right there, is the guy that tried to mine gold from under Genna during the fire. Some have suggested that he actually started it."

"Well, maybe that's the dark cloud that you have to deal with, but we need to get through the gate before they see us. Come on."

Reluctantly, James followed. As they reached the center of the bridge, he heard a shout from the garden. "They're getting away." Gavin shouted.

Donny and Garcia whipped around and raced to the bridge, guns raised but not firing. James watched as the second Sebastian followed their gauge, the archway to the garden closed up with Adon walled inside it.

Sebastian cursed as he turned back to face a blank wall, "Fuck!" then wheeled around to join the pursuit.

Seeing the whole group focus on them, James broke back into a sprint across the bridge. Suddenly, he heard a terrible thunder. He looked back and saw Adon appear once again beyond the wall. He was waving his hands back and forth, each time he did so, one of the wooden planks that James had already crossed blew off and fell into the abyss below the bridge.

Donny and Garcia skidded to a stop, short of the plunge and raised their weapons to stop their quarry. Donny fired a shot toward James, narrowly missing to the right. As he realigned his aim through the sight, a shout came from behind, "Stay that weapon, Donny. We need them alive!"

"How are we going to do that, Bas? The fucking bridge is gone."

James looked back from the path, surprised that no more shots had followed the first one. Turning back was his first mistake. He saw Gavin David's eyes open wide, in recognition. *Shit, he recognized me now.*

His second mistake followed immediately when his tongue moved far quicker than his brain. "You guys should do yourself a favor and toss Mister high and mighty Dah-veed off the bridge. Then we can all move on with our lives."

This verbal snark caused a sudden shift in the orders of restraint, apparently, when Gavin opened with a volley of shots from his own M-4. The other three took his cue and soon he had four weapons open up on him, on an open path along a cliff-face with no cover. A voice called out to him, no, that's not right. A voice spoke, seemingly from within his own head, not just any voice, but that of Adon. "Get through the gate, I can hold them off for now."

Despite the flurry of muzzle flashes and rifle reports echoing through the mountainside, none of the projectiles hit him. As a matter of fact, they seem to have been stopped short of him by some force. The still-pristine, unsmashed bullet slugs collected along the pathway. He knew that Adon had been responsible, but he had no idea how.

Although, since their brief talk with Adon, James had a feeling that he had no real idea about anything, not anymore. Nothing was as it seemed, and his mind wasn't taking it well. Even so, his body responded and he rushed into the opening to the cavern and followed Stuart up the ramp and through the gateway.

As soon as they were back in the familiar river-powered cavern, the Professor turned to James and was typically unflapped, "Well, that was somewhat unexpected."

"Which part, the unraveling of world history or the appearance of that lunatic Gavin and his henchmen... or the impromptu trip to Tibet?"

"Yes, that." He laughed. "We better get out of here before they figure out a way to get across that rope bridge."

"Yeah, we need to regroup. Do you still have the winch remote?"

"I do. Let's go."

They waded out to the winch cable and each took a good grip. Stuart hit the button and, in a moment, they were rushing against the current, through the tunnel.

Unbeknownst to them, Jones was still standing guard over the eccentric German linguist. At the sound of the winch-motor being activated, Jones went on high-alert and moved over to the water's edge waiting to see who came out of the tunnel; his weapon at the ready. As James and Stuart's heads popped out of the water, Fredrick made the move he had been waiting for. He rushed the soldier from behind and with a quick shove sent him over the edge and into the rushing water. The current swiftly carried the struggling soldier into the tunnel, as Fredrick went over to help Augustine and Angeline from the water.

James was aware of a splashing mass rushing past him, but couldn't tell what it was. With all of the things that didn't make sense, Fredrick being at the site didn't even phase him. Though the Professor immediately processed the anomaly.

"Fredrick, you son of a bitch. What the hell did you do?"

"It doesn't matter. I can't tell you how glad I am to see you two returning from the tunnel. I don't think that man was going to let me live out the day."

"It doesn't matter? It doesn't matter?" Stuart was incredulous. "Only three of us: James, myself, and you knew about the stone. So, imagine my surprise when four armed mercenaries showed up in Tibet. I know James didn't tell anyone. So, I ask you again. What did you do?"

Ever the detail-oriented German, Fredrick corrected him, "Well, technically, there were six mercenaries, or at least five plus the boss. But I took out the last one just now. Thank God they are all dead."

"Who said they were dead? And you still haven't answered the question."

"Wait, they aren't dead? Then let's get out of here. I will tell you everything in the car."

James interjected, "How did Gavin Dav-eed get involved in this, Fredrick? It was you, huh?"

"That's Gavin David? The one the Feds have been searching for? I never knew his name. I just had a number to call if anyone found any unusual mentions of gold, or golden cities." The fear was beginning to rise back into his voice. "Look, let's go. These are bad men. If they come back while we are standing here chatting, we're all dead. Please let's take the car and go."

James and Stuart exchanged a glance. Fredrick was right. They needed to get some distance and regroup. "Let's go." Stuart said, but as he approached his Range Rover, he noticed a new problem. All four tires were flat. "Crap."

Fredrick relished the opportunity to save the day again, hopeful that it would get him back into their good graces. "It's okay, I saw where Sebastian put his keys. We can take his vehicle. It's just over the ridge, over there."

James and the Professor shared a reluctant look, but resigned to the fact that they really had no choice. James looked over at the waypoint stone and noticed Fredrick's notes and the laptop. "Grab your stuff Fredrick, all of it."

They fast-walked down the path and over the hill. When they reached the two vehicles parked off the highway, Fredrick raced to the driver's side rear, reached under the wheel-well and found the keys.

James glanced at Stuart and nodded toward the second vehicle, Gavin's rental, "Should we return the favor? Do you have a knife on you?"

"No, I lost it somewhere along the way."

James pulled his sidearm from its holster and aimed it at the right front tire. Nanoseconds before he squeezed the trigger, Stuart grabbed his arm.

"Wait, I don't think we should do that. We want them to leave here, if they get out. We want them out looking for us. That will make it easier for us to come back, as long as we don't go anywhere that they would look for us. And one way or another we need to come back."

James nodded his understanding and holstered his weapon. But before turning to get into the SUV he planted a firm kick of his size-eleven hiking boots into the driver's door panel. *At least the rental company will make Gavin pay, even if we don't.* It was childish, he knew, but somehow it still made him feel better.

They climbed into the SUV, making Fredrick ride in the back seat, Augustine at the wheel and drove off, headed to the Boise area with no real destination in mind. They just needed to get away from this area and figure out their next move.

As the road noise became white noise, soothing their frayed nerves they settled in and reflected on the insane events of the day. The surreal nature of the journey to Tibet, followed by a run for their lives and the unexpected discovery of the involvement of Gavin David, not to mention the betrayal of Fredrick. It had been quite a day.

"So, what now, my fellow Traveler?" James broke the silence.

"I must admit, I don't even really know what just

happened so figuring out what is next is difficult. However, I don't think you and I should discuss the 'Traveler' portion of the story in front of Fredrick, because he clearly can't be trusted." Stuart's frustration and anger came out as bitterness as he stared at Fredrick in the rear-view mirror.

"I can't believe Gavin David popped up again. I was really hoping that his plane had crashed out in the Pacific."

"Yeah, what's the story there? I remember the news reports after the fire in Genna that they were looking for him, but I didn't pay that close of attention to it."

"Apparently, some contractor to the Town of Genna was doing core samples for a sewer system found some minerals that led them to believe that there was a large gold deposit under the ridge. Somehow, he reported those findings to Gavin David, who immediately threw like fifteen-million dollars at the project on the condition that he get all the mineral rights. I stumbled on the site, accidentally, and was captured by his crazy security guys. When the Sheriff came to rescue me, the whole thing unraveled and Mr. David went on the run. During the investigation it was discovered that he wasn't really looking for gold to mine. He was searching for something specific. He wasn't just mining for gold. He was searching for a place."

"Seven cities of gold?"

"Something like that."

"His kingdom." Fredrick interjected from the back.

"Kingdom?" Stuart asked.

"He thinks he's the heir to some kingdom. Fancies himself a king. Blowhard. He must've mentioned it, or 'fulfilling his destiny' a half dozen times that I heard."

Stuart thought about this, then asked, "Fredrick, it's about time for you to tell us what happened, but start with exactly what it was that he wanted you to report."

"I will get to why, but as far as what I was to report it was basically any references to Gold, Golden cities, Golden kingdoms and surprisingly diamonds. Especially, those within the last two-hundred-twenty years. I thought he was just a greedy prick looking for riches, but during the few hours I spent with him today, I realized it isn't that. He believes he is king of something and his people await the return of the rightful king. A Medieval-type of mentality."

"Diamonds? Stuart, he was looking for the gateway. And we led him right to it." James dug into his pocket and extracted the uncut diamond paperweight that Clark had left for them.

"However, he didn't seem to have found what he

was looking for in Adin, he seemed to only be chasing after us."

"Adin?" Fredrick called from the back seat. "I don't suppose there was a grand garden there, was there?"

James and Stuart both reacted, "Why?"

"Wait, there was? Holy crap, I was joking. Adin is an ancient reference to the Garden of Eden. I have never heard that term used for another place, though occasionally as a person's name. You found the Garden of Eden, in Idaho? No wonder nobody has ever found it. Who would have ever thought it was in Idaho? Amazing."

"It wasn't. Well, not exactly."

"James..." Stuart cautioned him. At this point, Stuart didn't trust his academic colleague on any level. In fact, he had been tempted to leave him behind to face whatever justice was coming his way. But the truth was, he really wanted to know why he had betrayed them.

"It's time Fredrick. I need to know what happened. I need a reason not to toss you out of the car alongside the road. Most importantly, I need the truth."

"I am sorry, my friend. I really felt bad about telling him, but I simply didn't have a choice. At least not one that wouldn't affect the safety of my family." Fredrick took a deep breath, and then fessed up about his gambling problem. He was clearly ashamed that he had put himself in this position. "So, after this man, Gavin, I never knew his name until today. But after this man, bought my debt from the Verducci brothers, I actually had a bit of a windfall and contacted him to pay off my debt. The next day, one of his men showed up at my office with a stack of pictures of my daughter and granddaughter. He proceeded to tell me that they weren't interested in my money, only my loyalty. If they ever found out that I had information that I failed to report, my girls would pay the price for my failure. I swear to you Stuart, if I had any other option, I would have taken it. You're my friend, but I still had to do it."

James looked to his neighbor, "What do you want to do?"

"Give him your phone."

"My phone?"

"Yes, Fredrick you need to call your daughter and have her go on a vacation for a few days while we settle this. Send them to Disneyland, or wherever. Let's remove that worry, so we can focus on our next steps. "

"What are those next steps?"

"I have no idea."

CHAPTER TWENTY-SEVEN

Gavin steamed as he drove down the highway. He couldn't believe that James Augustine had foiled his plan, yet again. He couldn't believe that the archaeologist, Angeline, and Augustine had outflanked his team. He couldn't believe that they had lost two men and had been forced to tightrope back to the portal. But mostly, he fumed because it didn't take him to the jungle of Hasabi, to his kingdom, but to some snowy mountain range.

"Who the hell was the guy with the flaming sword?" Donny said from the back seat, interrupting Gavin's thoughts.

"I don't know, but clearly Angeline and Augustine have figured out how to navigate the gate and this was one of the other portals. My Grandfather's journal spoke of seven portals, but he had set this one to stay open between our portal here and the jungle kingdom. We need them to figure out how to get where I am trying to go. Plus, once we do, I have something special in store for James 'Fucking' Augustine."

"What happened between you two?" Sebastian queried.

"He caused my exile. He stumbled onto another operation and that macho-man Sheriff Horne wouldn't stop sniffing around. I had to leave the country until the heat faded. He will pay for that. What a wonderful twist of fate that he inserted himself into this mission as well."

"Well, now that we know who he is, I will dig into his background and find some leverage, or at least have some idea what we are up against with him."

"Apparently, he is just some blowhard political consultant. He got lucky last time."

Donny, knew he should just let them talk, they were the bosses, he and Garcia were just grunts, but he simply couldn't contain himself. "Is anyone going to talk about what the fuck just happened? The Star Trek 'Beam me up Scotty' jump to another world to face the badass monk with the flaming sword and magic hands? We're just going to act like none of that happened?"

"It all happened, but none of it was our mission. Wrong place. The one part that was our business, we let flank us and escape, in part because you weren't on your game. So, sit back and shut it while I figure out what's next."

Sebastian was pissed at himself, for being side-tracked by Donny's fear. If they were both focused, perhaps the monk wouldn't have surprised them and they wouldn't have let the archaeologists escape. If he was honest, he was still shaken by the way the monk had looked right into him, as if he was searching his soul. He too, didn't understand much of what he saw there, but as the leader he couldn't be distracted by that. They still had a mission to complete, and it had just become more difficult. There had to be a way to figure out where Angeline and Augustine were headed. He needed more back-ground on Augustine, but Sebastian's computer was in the Suburban that they had stolen. He was help-less at the moment.

"Wait, that's it! I know how to find them." He dug his phone out of his pocket. "My drone is in the Suburban. It has a locate feature so that if you lose contact with it and it crashes, you can recover it. It is attached to the app that came with it. As long as the battery isn't dead, I should be able to track them."

He hurriedly opened the appropriate app and

input the PIN number that he had set up earlier. The app went through its connection process, which was agonizingly slow in the 3G data cell of such a rural area, but 3G was better than nothing. Once the icon showed that he was connected, he began to navigate to the locate function. The app itself was built to fly the drone, as a back-up to the remote control, and they had incorporated the locator function as something of an afterthought. So, while he quickly found the indicator showing that the locator was turned on, it took him several minutes to figure out how to actually use the function to locate the drone. Once he drilled down to the appropriate page, he clicked 'Find It' and the slow connecting process began again.

But this time, he expected to hit paydirt.

CHAPTER TWENTY-EIGHT

Only ten miles outside of Horseshoe Bend, the contemplative silence was broken. Fredrick had been using the laptop to continue working on translations, while James and Stuart had been silent and retrospective, thinking about the things that Adon had said, and the situation that they now found themselves in. Suddenly, an intermittent beeping sound began to eminate from the back.

"Fredrick, what's that beeping noise?" James asked, visibly irritated.

"I do not know. It is coming from the back."

"Well, find it and shut it off."

Fredrick climbed up and leaned over the back-seat trying to see if he could ascertain the source of the noise. Finally, he narrowed it down.

"It's coming from the large box underneath everything else. There are a lot of guns back here by the way, in case you were interested. But you're going to have to pull over to shut the beep off. I think the box says something about a drone, but I can't see much of it."

James perked up, "Guns... well, that's a lucky break."

"Crap, they are out of the portal."

"How do you know?"

"They are using the drone to try to find us. It's the only explanation that makes sense. Shit. Hang on."

Without waiting for them to do so, he skidded to a stop on the narrow shoulder of the road. James and Stuart jumped out and swung open the back doors, rapidly moving things aside to get to the box on the bottom. The box itself about two-feet by two-feet square and a foot deep. The two men slid it out and, as if communicating telepathically, they swung it right off the shoulder of the road and down the rocky bank into the Payette River. The current swiftly carried the box into the rapids and then it was gone.

"Track that Gavin."

They climbed back in the Suburban and took off down the highway.

"What is your dark cloud?" James asked Stuart.

"Well, I don't know for sure what Adon meant when he said that. I mean, I am sure that it has something to do with the find in Jerusalem. But I have no idea what I am supposed to face, or make right. The site is gone. It's all been classified. I don't have a specific person that I need to face, that I can think of. So, I am not sure." He paused in thought for a moment before continuing, "I do know one thing; we are going to face your cloud and stop Gavin David. Then we need to find a way to secure the site and find an easier way for use to access it without having to defy death every time we jump into that river. Then try to get back to Adon and clarify what is expected of me."

"We also need to find a way to make sure Fredrick keeps his mouth shut."

"He'll be fine. If we stop Gavin, there will be no more leverage to use against him." Stuart glanced at his friend in the rearview mirror. As they got into Horseshoe Bend, Stuart peeled off the road into the first gas station that he saw. Sliding to a stop in the loose gravel on the far side of the building.

"I'm not running from these guys. I don't like feeling that I am running away. Let's look and see what kind of weaponry we have and go take back our site."

"I was just thinking something similar." James looked across the highway at the rushing river. "If they are, indeed, tracking the drone, then they will follow it all the way into Emmett, assuming it doesn't get stuck in Black Canyon Reservoir. What if we find a place around here to hide out, once they go past us, we can just go back up to the portal site and get back to work. It's the last place they will look."

"And if they show back up, we'll be ready for them." Stuart concurred.

They backed the Suburban in on the side of a local sporting goods store with the hope that none of Gavin's team would even be looking for them up here as they raced after the drone's signal. Even so, each of them now had a weapon laid across their lap, just in case. Even Fredrick was given a firearm, though James had argued against it. Professor Angeline had forgiven Fredrick for his betrayal, after all if the situation had been flipped and it was his daughter and granddaughter in danger, he knew he would have told them whatever they wanted to hear to keep them safe.

Twenty minutes later, they saw Gavin's car zip past as they tried to catch up to the drone. Happy that phase one of their plan had worked, Stuart started the SUV and was about to take off when James stopped him.

"Let's run into the sporting goods store and see if there is anything that might help us, and maybe find a low profile dingy or Zodiak. With one of those attached to the winch, it sure will make for a more pleasant entry into the cavern." James said.

"Great idea. Let's go."

Ten minutes later, they loaded up the SUV and rolled up the highway. When they got back to the site, they drove the Suburban as far off the highway as they could go. Despite its SUV status, it clearly wasn't made for that terrain, like the Range Rover. They hoped, at minimum, that it wasn't as visible from the highway and wouldn't attract any attention.

They lugged the rubber boat over near the Range Rover and set Fredrick to work inflating it whilst James and the Professor went back for more cargo, weapons, and a couple of other potentially useful things that they had found at the Sporting goods store.

Once they got back, they attached the boat's rubber cleat to the winch-cable and dropped it into the water. They loaded it in a single layer of equipment and James laid down on top of it.

"Ready?" Stuart asked.

James gave him a thumbs up and the winch-motor whined as the cable unspooled, slowly allowing the watercraft to flow with the current into the stone scar.

Once inside, James hurriedly unloaded the raft

and pressed the remote for the winch, sending the boat back for his partners. They had decided to bring Fredrick into their confidence and bring him into the cavern. His skill with symbols might just prove valuable as they tried to decipher the symbols on the control panel of the portal.

While they had brought him in, they had also decided not to discuss their conversation with Adon. They were still trying to wrap their heads around that anyway, but it just felt like something that should be kept between the two of them. They had already slipped up by mentioning Adin and accidentally confirming the garden to him. Of course, neither of them had made the connection to Adin and Eden. The whole thing was too fantastical to believe, but they also knew, intuitively, that Fredrick had been correct. It was likely Eden, or at least the inspiration for the story of the Garden of Eden. They suspected that many of the stories in the history of mankind were about to be rewritten, at least for themselves. They desperately yearned for the truth, but they found themselves having a difficult time digesting the new truths that they had learned.

Needless to say, Fredrick was blown away by what he saw. They had chosen not to describe the cavern to him, but to let him experience it for himself. It was quite difficult to describe anyway, in any way that could do the place justice.

"My god! They've built a pyramid here, inside a mountain. How on earth did they do that?" Fredrick marveled. "Though I can see where the stories about the Seven Cities of Gold got their origins. This is also, likely that the inscriptions speak not of gold, but of golden or gilded things. The light makes them golden, not actual gold. Oh, this is fascinating." He said as he climbed the stairway.

James and Stuart watched quietly. Fredrick had a habit of talking to himself when he was processing something or trying to figure something out. They could tell that all of this monologue was rhetorical, and didn't require a dialogue. Professor Angeline also hoped that Fredrick's verbalization of the observations might just trigger something important in his own mind.

"Do you think there really are seven of them?" Fredrick asked off-handedly.

"Seven of what?" James replied.

"You know, Seven Cities of Gold. I wonder if there really are seven, or if that is just how the legend developed over the last three centuries."

Professor Angeline answered, "I haven't really had time to think about it. We know there are two. But most legends are based on truth of some level. The control panel has seventeen symbols that flash through, but that doesn't mean they are all locations. Plus, I can't imagine there would be seventeen of these without word getting out at some point. Still, as unlikely as it is that any of this exists, it is highly likely that there are more than two."

"Why don't we set up the trail cams and then go explore some of the other symbols and their associated locations." James suggested.

They had bought some trail cameras, which were motion activated, but in large part the reasoning behind the purchase of these particular trail cams was that they used a network to send you notifications and pictures once they were activated. Frankly, given who was chasing them, James would prefer claymores, just so they could be done with the running and the very real threat. But having notice that they were coming, would give them a much better chance than being blindsided like they had been before. They could choose to either evade, or attack, but at least with warning they would have choices.

"Should we put them in the cavern, or out by the tunnel entrance?" Stuart asked.

"It says that the average delay, or lag-time, between activation and receiving a message is two minutes, so I think we should put them outside the tunnel, that way, by the time they make their way into the cavern, we should know that they are here." He paused, then added, "In theory, anyway."

"Fredrick, why don't you watch the symbols on the panel while we go set up the warning system.

See if you recognize, or have insight to any of them. But for god's sake don't touch anything. You haven't really been briefed on what it does, yet."

Fredrick was already staring intently at the images as they flashed by. It was amazing, several looked similar to other symbols, yet they were just different enough to make any attempt at translation to be futile. "Will do." Came his reply as he watched the symbols float by. He recognized one that he had seen embroidered into Gavin David's notebook. He stood staring at it. It was an inverted pyramid with several strange markings on it, surrounded and cupped by three long leaves.

Augustine and Angeline rode the raft back up the mouth of the tunnel with the help of the winch. As they climbed ashore outside, James noticed that their eagle was watching them from his perch atop the pyramid. It seemed really interested in what they were doing, as they crawled around and installed one camera under the front bumper of the Range Rover, out of sight, but where anyone who was entering the tunnel would have to pass. They placed two more at various places overlooking the path. They then climbed back in the boat and let the cable lead them just inside the maw of the cave. James laid on his back as he fastened the camera onto the roof of the tunnel, ensuring that if anyone passed, they would know about it.

Finally, happy with the layout of the cameras, and having confirmed that they were connected to the app on his phone, the new Travelers floated back into the cavern. When they got up the stairs, it was immediately apparent that something was wrong.

Fredrick was gone.

CHAPTER TWENTY-NINE

Angeline and Augustine had played them. They hadn't even bothered looking along the way, as they watched the locator beacon follow their path toward where they lived in Emmett. Sebastian had located the drone, stuck in some reeds along the edge of Black Canyon Lake. A reservoir created by building a damn on the Payette River, which flowed through the dam and continued right into downtown Emmett. The ruse had worked. Sebastian had to give those guys some credit, they were resourceful. It was too bad that he would likely soon have to kill them. He had grown to admire their tenacity and ability to adapt to surprising changes in their situation.

Gavin David, had no such admiration for them, indeed his hatred for James Augustine bordered on the same level of obsessiveness as his talk about being the rightful heir of some mysterious kingdom. His frustration at being duped only increased his sense of entitlement, as if the two academics had some personal vendetta against him. It was all fantasy, of course. Sebastian could see that they had had no idea that his team was on to them until they had crossed the bridge in the mountains and attacked with guns blazing. Sebastian would have to keep a close eye on Mr. David, his instability, already excessive, had grown even worse since the portal didn't take them to his kingdom as he had led them all to believe. Sebastian briefly wondered whether it existed at all.

Of course, it really didn't matter what he thought. Mr. David called the shots and paid the bills. Paid them quite handsomely, too. But payday or no payday, if Gavin put them in position to lose anyone else on the team, Sebastian resolved to take him out if necessary. It would suck, he had only been paid half of his fee, but he would do it if he had to.

"Faster, faster! We have to stop them." David barked repeatedly, as Sebastian screamed the car up the valley at near-redline, once again to try to catch the two archeologists.

He decided to bait Gavin, a bit. "These academics sure are resourceful. They outflanked us on the mountain, escaped in our vehicle, and now duped us so that they could double back to the portal. I wonder what they are doing up there, now. Surely, they didn't go back to visit the guy with the flaming sword. Where do you think they went?"

"I don't fucking care where they went, but I will make sure that they know what Hell feels like when we get to them. Just get us there." Gavin growled.

CHAPTER THIRTY

James and the Professor rushed down the ramp, into the cavern. The M-4 rifles that they had pilfered from the SUV dangled from shoulder slings. Within just a few steps they realized that this wasn't the cavern in the Himalayas, similar, but quite different. The equipment and the pyramidic structure were pretty much the same, though there was no obvious power source here, like there were in the other two caverns that they had been to. Some kind of animal had made a bed for itself beneath the equipment. And then, of course, the two human skeletons laying askew in front of the tunnel to the side confirmed that this was someplace new.

"Damn it! I told him not to touch anything. What the hell was he thinking?"

"Probably the same thing we were thinking when we went through the first time. We had no idea what to expect, but we went anyway. He, at least, knew that we and most of Gavin's goons had survived the trip. That's more information than we had."

The two headed for the tunnel opening. They paused briefly to look at the skeletal remains on the ground. "How long do you figure these guys have been here, Professor?"

"A long time. They are pretty well preserved in this cave, but I would guess at least a couple of hundred years. What's left of their clothing seems reminiscent of the robes the Tibetan people wear, though not nearly as advanced as the one Adon wore."

"Interesting, could there be more than one portal there?"

"I suppose there could be, since ours seemed only to deliver us to the Garden of Adin." He nodded to the tunnel, "Let's go find out."

The two wound their way outward, the humidity increasing with each step. Before they even reached the end, it was clear that, no, they weren't back in Tibet. The air was hot and heavy, and the smell of meat cooking reached them, perking up their nerves as they knew they would find people on the other side. James swung his rifle up into ready position as he saw light at the end of the tunnel.

He made eye contact with the Professor, who had also made his weapon ready. "Ready? You go left, I will go right."

He counted down with the fingers on his left hand; three, two, one. They spun out onto the pathway clearing both sides before even noticing the view ahead of them; it certainly wasn't the Himalayas. It looked more like Jurassic Park. The jungle's canopy spread as far as the eye could see. A small village sat below them and to the right. A blur ran from the village into the jungle, followed by seven dark-skinned warriors of some kind.

"That has to be Fredrick that they are chasing. Let's go get him."

Angeline and Augustine jogged down the path and into the village with their eyes peeled for any additional warriors. James slowed to a stop as he found something quite different. At the edge of the village stood a large tiger carved from white stone. The level of detail was impressive. Just past it, villagers were gathering around them. Instinctively they raised their weapons, but one look in their eyes and he knew that their intent wasn't malice. Several closest to him fell to the ground and began genuflecting, praying, worshiping. At first, James thought that they had walked into some sort of worship ritual for the tiger statue, but as he went to walk around them to go after Fredrick, he realized that the villagers kept shifting too, so that they were always facing him.

But why would they worship me? Do they worship everyone that comes through the portal? If they did, then why are they chasing Fredrick into the jungle.

"I think I know why?" Stuart interrupted. He pointed to an adobe wall adjacent to the path.

James turned to see what he was pointing at... it was him. Well, not exactly him, but a painting on the wall depicting a man walking alongside a white tiger. The man's left foot was smashing a king's crown into the dirt on the ground. James had to admit, despite the crude painting, the man did bear a remarkable resemblance to himself. The symbolism was clear, this man had dethroned a king. The less clear idea, at least from the painting's perspective, was that in doing so he had freed these people.

"I wonder who he was. Or when he was here." James pondered.

"Either way, perhaps the likeness will cause them to leave us be while we go get Fredrick."

James awkwardly half-waved at the villagers, uncertain how to act, as he backed away and followed the path, he had seen Fredrick and the warriors take, into the jungle. It got very dark, very quickly once he got out of the clearing of the path. But he could hear them running about one-hundred-yards up from where he was. He followed the sound and picked up his pace; the professor kept right on his tail. Dodging fallen trees and hidden roots they bounded through the jungle at full-speed, then burst into a clearing and saw that four of the warriors had Fredrick pinned to the ground, the others were standing around them watching eagerly.

James fired a three-shot burst from his M-4 up into the treetops. The echo boomed through the clearing and everyone froze instantly. The Professor stepped out beside James and spread out to the right; muzzle aimed at the warriors.

Suddenly, one of the warriors on the fringes gasped audibly and dropped to his knees causing the others to look up at James and follow suit.

"Fredrick, are you okay?"

"I am now, thankfully." He said as he stood up and brushed himself off, breathing rapidly after the long chase.

"Didn't I tell you not to touch anything?"

The front door to the house on the clearing opened and a guard immediately rushed at James, clearly not buying the worshiping thing that the other guards were doing. His eyes spoke of anger and hatred.

Ten feet from James, the look of anger and hatred morphed into one of fear. He skidded to a stop and began to slowly backpedal. Stuart had whipped his weapon around in James direction as well. James turned slowly to see what had spooked both men.

A large albino tiger strolled up beside him, just like he had seen in the painting. It roared at the other men, causing them to retreat a bit further, eyes wide with fear. The tiger turned to James who had been as still and unmoving as possible, playing dead, but on his feet. The beast pushed his forehead into James' thigh and rubbed back and forth. Not knowing what else to do in yet another bizarre situation, he reached down and began petting the top of its head and gave it a scratch behind its ear. Such a strange sound when a beast with the power to kill everyone in the clearing, purrs like a kitten.

A voice called out from the front of the large house, "Well, if Zanzibar trusts you, then so shall I."

"Zanzibar? Is he a pet?"

"No, not at all. The late king named him that when he had him chained in captivity. Meant to display his virility, or some such nonsense." The woman replied. She was tall, lean, and fair-skinned with long red hair, speckled with an occasional gray hair. She wore a golden broach in her hair and a necklace depicting a great tree. She looked at James, "You really do look like, you know. But then, they didn't spend any real time with him. I know you aren't him, but if Zanzibar has warmed to you, then I am happy you are here. My name is Vanna. They call me Queen, but I want no such title, I am simply a leader of my people. Why are you here?"

"Who do I look like?"

"Will. It's been many, many years, but despite some small differences, you look like him."

"Will? Hmpf. At any rate, I am James Augustine, this in my colleague Professor Stuart Angeline. And we mean you no harm. We simply came here to retrieve our wayward friend here, Fredrick."

"You came here with your boomsticks and expect me to believe you just believe that your 'friend' found his way to the Hasabi Kingdom accidentally? That you don't want anything more?"

"I do, it's the truth." James replied.

"Wait, did you say Hasabi Kingdom?" He looked at James and Stuart, "This is the place the Gavin David has been looking for. I heard him mention the Hasabi villagers while we were in the car. Oh man, that's why his journal had the symbol on it."

"Gavin Dah-veed? He's coming here?" for the first time a glimmer of fear shone in her eyes.

"I don't know, but he has been looking for it for a long time. He kept referring to himself as the rightful heir to some kingdom and something about diamonds. Do you know him?"

"No, but our late-King Andres Dah-veed once ruled these lands. He captured me as a child and raised me as a slave in his household." She began shaking, not with fear, but hatred. "The things he did to me, to everyone here are unspeakable. He would only allow the villagers to eat meat twice a month, and the meat was always who he deemed to be the weakest amongst them. If they are related, then he must be a very evil man."

"He raised you? But Gavin called him his great-great-great-great grandfather. That can't be possible. How old was he? When did he die?"

"He was King for one-hundred-thirty years. But Will Clark killed him, finally, with the help of Zanzibar."

"Wow, that's a long time, especially out here in the jungle. Wait, what? Will Clark?" James offered.

"Yes, he and some man named Meri... something. I never could pronounce his name.

"But that's not possible, that would have been over two-hundred-fourteen years ago."

She cupped the tree pendant hanging around her neck in one hand, "Yes, that sounds about right. I never did understand how Andres' calendar worked."

Stuart noticed it first, then James saw it too. The golden metal that formed the tree began to disform around the grasp of her hand. It was made from the metal in the caverns. *Could this be possible?*

"And the villagers, have they been alive since the

time of Andres, too?" The professor asked trying to understand how this lovely young woman could be more than two-hundred years old.

"What is this talk about diamonds?" James interjected.

"No, the villagers seem to live normal life cycles. I am not sure why Zanzibar and I have lived so long. As for diamonds, they are the reason Andres' became a monster. The villagers who were not fit to be warriors and guards, were sent to work in the diamond mine. One of the first things that I did after Andres died was release them from that bondage and shut down the mine. The jungle has overtaken it now, I doubt that the villagers today even know it is there."

Gunshots, echoed through the valley, lots of them.

"Vanna, do your warriors have boomsticks?"

She shook her head.

"Gavin and his men are here. Have these warriors go into the house with you and protect you. We will go help the villagers. Fredrick come with us." James handed the linguist one of his guns, a Beretta PX4 Storm forty caliber handgun. "Do you know how to use this?"

"Not well, but I have shot a few times."

"Zanzibar," He scratched his ears, "We could use your help, too."

The majestic beast seemed to understand perfectly as he darted off into the Jungle. The three explorers raced after him, hoping that the volley of shots they had heard were for intimidation and not slaughtering the villagers.

CHAPTER THIRTY-ONE

"This is it. This is my kingdom." Gavin shouted as they walked out of the cavern. The four men, well-armed and still frustrated at being duped by Angeline and Augustine jogged down the path toward the village.

Three warriors stepped out of the jungle foliage and moved to block their path, carrying spears and daggers. Sebastian let loose a volley of gunfire over their heads into the trees. He wasn't prepared to kill anybody...yet, though there was a list of potential personal scores to settle. No, his job now was simply to secure the site and find out how things would work out with the would-be king. The three warriors scrambled out of sight.

"Warning shots only, for now. Do not engage directly, unless you are directly fired upon. Got it?"

"Yes, Sir." Replied Garcia and Donny, in unison.

Gavin, however, wanted to establish his dominance. He was a king after all, their King, whether they liked it or not. He opened fire into the jungle where the three warriors had scattered into, spraying an entire magazine into the spot. He was rewarded with one scream and a thud as something fell in the underbrush.

Down in the village, people scrambled to grab children and find cover. Gavin threw a few shots in their general direction for good measure.

Sebastian stopped short and reared around into Gavin's face. "Sir, we are not slaughtering innocents. That's not what I signed on for."

"They are the descendants of slaves, my slaves. My miners. Get out of my face, or you will be their dinner." He saw the questioning expression in Sebastian's eyes. "Yes, these 'innocents' as you call them are cannibals. Didn't I mention that? We will teach them a lesson on submission, or you will be their next meal. Understood?"

Donny and Garcia shared a glance, then looked to Sebastian for orders. It was clear by the bloodlust glaring from their benefactor's eyes that he had snapped. The three soldiers, while not always model citizens, had always, always fought for freedom of the people, not their oppression and enslavement. Sure, the lines were blurred occasionally, and they had stolen property that wasn't theirs along the way.

We are not saints... but neither are we cold-blooded murderers. Donny thought to himself. *But then again, Gavin was correct, cannibals do pose an unnatural threat and are not to be taken lightly.*

They kept walking down the path, the three looking sullen and less confident than they had mere moments ago. Sebastian was moments away from turning on his boss, but that would mean that the men didn't get paid. Of course, if they stayed, they had been promised riches of unimaginable pro-portions.

"Go drag them all out into the center of the vil-lage, so I may address them," Said Gavin in his most imperial tone. The remaining three soldiers hustled ahead.

"This guy is nuts." Whispered Garcia as they ran.

"Just do your jobs, so we can get paid and get out of here. If he crosses the line, then I will deal with it. Understood?" Sebastian replied.

Gunfire opened up behind them, the three spun around ready to face their adversaries, only to see Gavin pouring bullet after bullet into a mural of a man and a tiger. Finally, his magazine ran dry and the pockmarked wall was in shambles. They watched Gavin look up at the statue of the tiger and reach for a new magazine. They could see where this was going, Gavin had finally snapped.

A white blur raced from the jungle and tackled Gavin, flinging him across the path into the foliage on the other side. Sebastian, Garcia, and Donny started to run back up to save the boss.

"Don't even think about it." Came a voice from directly behind them.

James and Gavin hit the ground rolling, momentum carrying them off flat ground and over the rim of a steep grade, littered with dead leaves and foliage, which caused them to slide and roll and tumble down the hill. Now and again they tumbled into each other creating a bruised, bloody mess, though neither one of them had any control of the slide and neither could gain an advantage over the other. Gravity ruled.

After what seemed like forever, but was likely only ten or twelve seconds, they hit the bottom and as the ground flattened out, they came to an abrupt halt with a thud. For a brief moment neither of them moved as they lie gasping for air and grasping at consciousness. Both men seemed to realize what had happened at the same moment and jumped up to finish the other. Gavin kicked at James' midsection and jarring his foot into his ribcage. The kick hurt, but James was ready for the opening that it left him and sent a powerful right cross into Gavin's cheek, knocking him off balance and tipping him to the ground. Before he could get back to his knees, James was straddled on top of him, MMA-style, raining blows down until his hands hurt.

Gavin David's men had been so caught up watching Gavin's antics that none of them were watching their rear. Now they were taken by surprise, and in a very tight spot. Bas looked at Garcia and received a nod in return. They didn't know much about their quarry, but they did know that the archaeologist and the linguist had never served in the U.S. military. They didn't have enough info on Augustine to rule it out completely.

The decision was made, three soldiers versus two academics. Even in their bad position, they still had the advantage. Sebastian held three fingers up in front of his body. The countdown began: three, two...

Bullets flew between them and around their feet, causing all of them to jump. "I said Don't even try it. Now drop your weapons, before my aim improves."

Garcia and Donny dropped their rifles and raised their hands in the air. Sebastian hesitated. Just then up ahead James Augustine stepped out onto the path dragging a bloodied Gavin David with him.

"Enough, drop them, now!" James shouted.

Sebastian had had about enough; he wasn't one to quit. *That little shit has meddled in our affairs for the last time.* While the other two went down to their knees, Sebastian dropped his rifle to the ground. Every pair of eyes watched it fall which gave him the spit second to pull the folding FMG out from under his shirt and aim it at James.

Something slammed into his body, throwing him to the ground with a thud. He looked up and saw a snarling albino tiger, just like the statue, staring down at him with its paws on his chest, daring him to move.

"Zanzibar!" Called James, "Good boy. Come here. I don't want anyone to die if we can avoid it."

The cat gave a growl, then a roar into Sebastian's face, he felt wetness trickle down his legs as his bladder let go. The beast pushed off his chest with a huff and pranced over to where James was.

"Fredrick, would you be so kind as to gather up their weapons?"

Queen Vanna stepped out onto the path, surrounded by her personal guard, and walked directly up to Gavin David and looked him up and down, then dismissed him completely. "You are clearly not even a shadow of the man Andres was. Yes, you have his evil streak, but your insecurities obscure any potential goodness within you." She looked at her head guard and said something to him in Hasabi.

James had no idea what she said, but did not interfere when two of her guards walked up and grabbed the never-would-be king and walked him into the center of the village. Villagers had begun to peek their noses out now that the gunfire had abated. They watched as the guards dragged Gavin over to the cooking pit and roughly threw him down on the grate, and tied his hands & feet to it with woven reeds. One of the men then sprinkled him with salt.

Vanna walked over and grabbed a torch from the gazebo and carried it over to the cooking pit. Gavin squirmed against his bonds vigorously.

"You can't do this!"

"So, Gavin Dah-veed, you thought that you could walk in here after two hundred years and waltz right into your grandfather's seat?"

"I am the rightful heir to this kingdom!"

"Rightful? Really? Let me tell you what you have a right to. You have a right to stay in your own world, though you seem to have given up that right. You have the right to NOT enslave my people. You have the right to face the same punishment that your grandfather dished out on those that displeased him." She paused and waved the torch before placing it under the grate. "You have the right to join us for dinner."

Gavin started to whimper and squirm as he felt

the heat, rolling from one side to the other. Steam began to rise from the grates causing his gyrations to intensify and his whimpers turned to screams.

James and Stuart were laughing at his pathetic sniveling, not because they enjoyed seeing someone burn, but because they saw something that Gavin could not. Queen Vanna had lain the torch in the empty fire chamber so Gavin would feel the heat, but once she was certain that she had his attention she kicked it with her foot, into a pail of water. The steam made it all seem more real and had sent the 'rightful heir' into a tizzy.

"You should also know that my people ended their cannibalistic ways the very day Andres was killed. It was his evildoing, not theirs."

It took Gavin more than a few seconds to understand what she had said, to realize that he wasn't being cooked. In fact, he hadn't even been burnt at all.

"My people, the Hasabi, are not slaves, or miners, or subjects of the realm. They are people. They are farmers and craftsmen. They are mothers and fathers, sons and daughters. They do not even know that a diamond mine once existed. I made sure of it. I have watched over them for all of these years, since even before Andres died. I will not allow them to go back to that existence. Have I made myself clear?"

"I'm sorry. So sorry." He said under his breath.

"Sorry for what? Aside from destroying a painting of my friend, Will, and his friend, Zanzibar, you have accomplished nothing. But I know, and so do all of these men, what your intent was. It was evil. So, the question is, what do we do with you?"

"I have a thought, your highness..."

"Stop that, I am simply Vanna."

"Very well, Vanna. I know that the authorities in our homeland will be most eager to ensure that he finds justice, or, at least, a prison cell. If he agrees not to fight us or the charges, and agrees to never discuss the existence of this place or the portal, I would be willing to take him back and turn him over to them." James offered.

"And what of the other three?"

Sebastian spoke up, "We were just hired guns. The man is certifiably insane. I was ready to take him out myself if he decided to attack the villagers, I told these two that just moments before all of this happened. Ask 'em, they'll tell you."

Vanna thought for a moment, then turned to her head guard, "Cut him loose."

Gavin stood shakily and tried to gather his composure. He dusted off his khaki pants and wiped the tears, blood, and snot from his face with the back of his hand. He didn't have many options left. Though he had enough money that he would at least be able to obtain a good lawyer for the trial. The thought didn't make him feel any better. He had lost. There were no diamonds to be had and the kingdom seemed to be out of reach, and honestly, without the diamonds why would he want to live in this dump even if he was the King.

His eyes went first to Vanna, then narrowed when they found James Augustine. The man was responsible for the position that he was in. *If it wasn't for him, this whole thing would have gone down quite differently.*

He nodded, in acquiescence to Vanna and walked over to join the group of men on the path.

Vanna called out to Sebastian and his men, "You three, there is nothing for you here. There are no diamonds or any other reason for you to return. If you do, I promise it will not end peacefully."

"We were never here." Bas stated flatly.

Her guards surrounded the four men and Fredrick, while Vanna walked over to speak with James and Stuart. "It was a pleasure to meet you. It is amazing how much you resemble Will. I hope you are as good a man as he was."

"I didn't know him, but I am constantly striving to be a better man than I was yesterday."

"Thank you both." She pulled out a small cloth bag tied with twine and handed it to Stuart. "Perhaps you can use this to better secure the portal from your side, but you will both always be welcome here." She gave each man a kiss on the cheek.

Stuart, opened the bag and looked inside. It contained a dozen or so golf ball sized rough cut diamonds. He showed James what it was. "Yes, I think this will be more than adequate. We will protect it. Thank you." They turned to rejoin the rest of the men for the walk home.

James called back, "Thank you, my Queen. May you and your people live in peace, again."

The guards escorted them part way up the path then stopped forming a line across the trail. The message was clear, there is no turning back.

James led the four men up the path, Fredrick walked alongside them and Stuart and Zanzibar brought up the rear, keeping an eye on them. His mind calm for the first time in what felt like ages. It had been a whirlwind of activity over the last several days, full of fascinating events and dangerous situations. But Stuart knew that his troubles hadn't started then. No, the dis-ease in his mind began more than two years ago, and he hadn't really gotten over it, nor had he really tried to deal with it. He had made, arguably, the biggest archaeological find of the last three thousand years only to, not only have it taken away from him, but to have the historic site nuked and erased from the history books. It was, in his mind, a crime against humanity. But it seemed rewriting history had become the new trend, especially in America, but around the world too. He had felt the same shame watching people tear down statues in town squares because people were suddenly sensitive to what had happened over a century ago. Instead of remembering our past, good and bad, and learning from it, the trend was now about destroying it and pretending that those things never happened. Removing those lessons from our history and evolution as a society would undoubtedly be a bad thing for humanity in the long-term. He knew that this was the black cloud that Adon had mentioned, but he was at a loss as to what he was supposed to do about it.

He glanced back at the villagers who were all gathered on the path watching them leave. Suddenly, Gavin tripped and stumbled into Fredrick who was knocked to the ground. Gavin came away from the collision holding the Beretta that they had given Fredrick.

Gavin held the pistol to Fredrick's head while his other arm wrapped around his neck. Hiding behind the German linguistics expert, he ordered everyone to put down their weapons. The warriors complied, dropping their spears in the dirt, as did Stuart Angeline, out of concern for his friend.

To their credit, none of Gavin's men made a move to escape the unarmed warriors, but stood still in place. Perhaps it was out of self-preservation as they all eyed James, who was unwilling to relinquish his firearm.

"Drop it, now." Gavin yelled.

"No, let Fredrick go. It's not him you have a beef with, it's me. Take me instead. If you let him go, I will drop my weapon and submit myself to you."

"You will do what I asked, or I swear to god I will pull the trigger in five, four, three..."

James had nothing more to bargain with. While he didn't fully trust Fredrick, he also didn't want his stubbornness to be the reason that he was killed. He had nothing more to offer other than himself, but the madman had ignored that offer. He dropped the rifle out of his hands and let it hit the ground.

Gavin continued to shuffle backwards up the path, dragging Fredrick with him. As the path curved, he had to repeatedly glance behind him to make certain that he wasn't walking himself off the edge. When he looked back, James had made his move.

In the split second that Gavin glanced away, James reached under his shirt and drew the 9mm S&W Shield from its conceal carry holster and aimed it two-handed at Gavin's head as he marched forward to close the gap. When Gavin looked back, his eyes went wide in surprise.

"Augustine!" he bellowed as he swung his weapon toward James, releasing his hold on Fredrick.

Zanzibar saw the madman's intent and sprang into action. He leapt more than ten feet and swiped a paw across Gavin's arm, opening the flesh to the bone, as his jaws clamped onto the back of the man's neck. In less than a second, Gavin's last gasp at revenge died. Moments later, so did he; killed by the same paw that had ended the reign of King Andres, more than two hundred years ago.

Zanzibar walked away, nonchalantly, and brushed past James on his way into the cavern. By the time the men reached the cavern, Zanzibar was stretched out across his bed, resting his head on the base of the machine, and its glittering golden metal contoured to cup his head as he dozed off, snoring steadily and evenly.

CHAPTER THIRTY-TWO

Three Weeks Later

The TV in the corner of the diner flashed the 'Breaking News' scroller across the bottom proclaiming a 'significant, yet controversial, archaeological discovery has government agencies backpedaling'. James and Stuart ate their sandwiches as they waited for the story to break. It had already broken on social media and several websites this morning, but this was the first broadcast story that they had seen. It would definitely be interesting to see how it played out. They had brainstormed how to address it for days, now they toasted the culmination of their plan, Stuart with a Corona clinked James' glass of iced tea.

Stuart's home had been 'broken into' a few days after they had returned from the Hasabi Kingdom. Stuart had, of course filed a police report, but strangely the only things taken were an old laptop and a bunch of thumb-drives.

James spent several days sitting in the main library at Boise State University, compiling the data and pictures. He was there for several reasons, first to muddy the I.P. address for the submission, and to give James and Stuart some distance from each other while the Feds breathed down Stuart's neck over the security breach and the possible breach of contract, but also because there were assets to be utilized at the campus. Once they realized that Google Earth's image of the coordinates had been altered, likely at the behest of one of the governments involved. James had reached out to Fredrick once again. He gave him the coordinates and asked him to find someone that could get him a satellite picture. Trust was still an issue for James, at least where Fredrick was concerned, but even he had to admit that the linguist had made great strides toward restoring that trust. Still, James gave him only the coordinates, no other information. This project had to remain exclusively between Angeline and Augustine in order to pull it off and keep Stuart from landing in some secret federal prison cell. True to form, Fredrick was back within just a few hours with multiple photos of the site, including zoomed shots which still showed scorched marks around the opening, even two years later. It completed the package that he put together which included photos from inside the temple grounds and a narrative of the entire find. He attached it all to an email and hit send. It was done.

Stuart's conscience was cleared, even if his legal status was in doubt, and he smiled as the CNN broadcaster came back from commercial.

"The ironically well-known hacker group, Anonymous, broke a story today about what sounds like an amazing archaeological find in the middle east. The story suggests that the true center of the Old Testament, the original site of Jerusalem, including a well-preserved Temple of Solomon, was discovered more than two years ago and was subsequently destroyed via, get this, a tactical nuke. The pictures included in the release painted a compelling argument. CNN correspondent, Jessy Draper asked the State Department spokesman, Deborah Schuster about it, and here is what she had to say, and I quote: 'Wouldn't that be cool, not some minor temple, but the Temple of Solomon himself... But no, the story is a complete hoax, photoshopped images the whole works. I mean do you really think that a nuke could go off in the middle east, and nobody would know about it?' end quote. And in other news..."

Stuart laughed, "Well, that didn't take long. Anonymous will fight back, but that was always going to be the government's response to this. But the story is out there, some will believe it, some won't. But it's the truth either way."

"I'd have said it was crazy, had I not seen all the crazy that I have seen over the last few weeks. Now I think it's fascinating. Thanks for letting me be part of getting it out to the world."

Stuart pushed his chair back from the table, "You ready to go?"

"Absolutely."

Less than two hours later they pulled the Range Rover off the highway and with the press of a button the gate swung open. Once they were through, it closed automatically behind them. They had sold off a couple of the diamonds that Vanna had given them, which had brought them enough capital to buy this piece of property, just under eighty acres, and the water rights. It was an important step toward securing the portal, by owning the land, they could fence it off, gate the driveway which now allowed them to easily drive all the way to the tunnel opening. A large forklift, many, many ratchet straps, and no small amount of sweat had been needed to relocate the Waypoint Stone, clearing the pathway. It was coming along nicely. A large well-insulated steel building had been erected, it butted right up against the mountain. Inside there were sleeping quarters, a kitchen, a makeshift library, a laboratory, and a warehouse area which stored all the tools, devices, and weapons that they might need as they explored the portal's capabilities. The Waypoint Stone had been placed at the center of the library, which at this point only contained historical and language reference books from Stuart's home collection, but was destined for growth as they moved their operations here.

On the far end of the warehouse portion was a newly installed vault door, designed to be impenetrable. They had cut a hole into the side of the mountain and installed the door, the days of floating down the river to reach the portal were over.

Angeline and Augustine had not used the portal since the trip to the jungle with Gavin David and his crew, not for lack of desire, for that was nearly all that they could think about. They really had no idea what being a Traveler meant, or what it would entail. But the truth is that they needed the break. They needed to deal with their past so that they could move forward onto whatever path they were taken.

Once the news had aired Stuart's discovery of Jerusalem, they decided that their hiatus was over, it was time to go back up the ramp and get answers. They were as prepared as they could be given that they had no idea what to expect next.

James placed his palm on the palm reader causing the door to buzz briefly, then swing outward. "Let's go."

They climbed the stairs and went to the machine that they were now calling the 'Key Generator' and watched the symbols flash by on the screen. When the appropriate one showed up, an odd, grainy teardrop shape, Stuart reached out and grabbed it off the screen, then walked it over to the glowing screen on the portal and held it up until the screen grabbed the key and the gate hummed to life. Together they walked up the ramp and with a flash of light and a slight breeze they walked down again into the cavern. They skirted the familiar lava pool and walked directly to the hidden crevice which led them out into the cold mountain air. It was nighttime in Tibet, but they could see light emanating from the garden as they walked down the stairs and over the, now repaired, wood plank bridge.

"How do you feel about this?" James asked.

"Both eager to get answers, and afraid of what those answers might be. I have always thought history was fairly accurate, though specific details were skewed at times. Adon shattered much of that belief last time in the few short minutes that we spent with him."

"I get that, I'm a history geek, too. But my biggest concern is that he has us mistaken for someone else, I'm not Odin, or Jesus for crying out loud. And you are a great guy, but I doubt you are a Saint, ya know what I mean?"

"I do, I guess time will tell. And now seems to be the time" Stuart replied as they approached the archway. They strolled down the winding path, and just like the first time, Adon was seated in meditation at the base of the great tree.

James noticed something that he hadn't seen before, the symbol that was the key to this portal, the grainy teardrop shape was centered on the tree just above Adon's head. It was a natural knot in the tree, that had been taken as the symbol for the, what was it... realm? James pointed it out to Stuart in a whisper so as not to disturb Adon's meditation. They quietly took their seats on the modified stumps and waited.

"So, you made the choice to come back. Interesting."

"You made it sound like we were chosen, or something. I thought it was preordained, or our destiny."

"Yes, you are chosen. But no, we would never force someone into this life, it must come from within. The Traveler must emerge from who you already are." Adon looked over his shoulder at them. "I see that your black clouds are gone. That is good for you. And, Professor, the truth is always the way, whether people accept it or not."

"I have to admit that I kind of wished that they had accepted it, otherwise I don't see how it changes anything for them, or for me."

"Change is very difficult, but change is inevitable. You will have to change your understanding of a few things, that is difficult too. James, tell me how you felt when your black cloud lifted."

"I was glad that we were done running for our lives, but I did wish he didn't have to die."

"Ah, you think that he was your black cloud? Hmmm. What if I told you that he had nothing to do with your black cloud? That your black cloud was all within you. It was the resentment that you held against him for the fire and for taking advantage of people afterward. The resentment was your black cloud, once he died so did your resentment, which is good. People sometimes hold on so tightly that even after it's gone, they cannot let it go. However, if he had never existed, but you still went through the same experience with the fire, you would likely have placed your resentment on something else, the power company, the government, God. That is often part of the grieving process, but until you can let it go, you cannot really begin to heal. Holding on to a resentment is like taking poison and hoping the other person dies. It is normal, yet it is not healthy for you. Do you understand?"

James did understand. He had been working through how he reacted to situations and things that happen in life, throughout his sobriety. It had been so clear to him, and his self-awareness had been keen enough to catch those resentments, but where Gavin David was concerned, it had never occurred to him. A blind spot in the wake of tragedy. "Yes, I think I do. I thought my self-awareness had improved greatly over the last six years. Apparently, I have a ways to go."

"Don't we all. Let me ask, do you meditate and/or pray?"

"I pray all the time, throughout every day. I use to meditate, but that has slipped since the fire. Why?"

"You already know the answer. Without meditation your self-awareness suffers. For how can you speak up and pray for guidance, yet never slow down and quiet yourself enough to hear the answers? "

"Good point."

Stuart spoke up, "So, a linguistics friend of ours overheard us use the word Adin, I promise we weren't trying to tell him about this place. Anyway, he seems to think that this is the Garden of Eden. Is it? What's the story of the garden?"

"The is the Garden of Adin, but most myths, legends, and stories aren't made up, not completely. They are usually based on some nugget of truth. Like what I told you about Odin and Poseidon, many elements of the story are true, but man tends to fill in details to embellish the story."

"So, does that make this the Tree of Knowledge?"

"The Vikings called it Yggdrasil. As I told you on your last visit, all life springs from this garden, as does all knowledge."

"Yggdrasil? As in the tree that connects the nine worlds, and burns to set off Ragnarök?"

"In days past, some Travelers tried to gain followers by telling stories about this place, but over the years the stories morph into something different. The gates connect different lands and cultures, not the tree, but you can see, now that you have been through the gates how back in those days it would feel like different worlds. A Norseman might arrive here without too much shock because it is snowy and mountainous, but if he went through the gate to, say, the desert or the jungle; would it not seem like a different world? But there is another part of the Yggdrasil myth that is more pertinent to your journey."

"What's that?"

"It was said that the gods assemble at Yggdrasil daily, essentially as governing bodies. As I have said, some Travelers have been seen as gods, but the meetings were not about governance of the people, they were about governance of their own minds and spirits. They would come and meditate and center themselves so they would be in the best frame of mind as they went out into the world to spread love, peace and freedom. And also, to seek advice and guidance, occasionally they even followed that advice." He smiled, as if remembering some specific event, "Some, however, succumbed to the god-like status and lost their way. These are simply humans, being a traveler doesn't lead you to perfection, the fallible nature of man is ever-present and their weaknesses can be cunning, baffling, and powerful."

"Was Andres David a Traveler?"

"No, on only a handful of occasions, in all of history, people have found the chambers and figured out how to utilize a portal, often that became driven by greed, as they had the advantage of being able to traverse the globe. Today, with man's advancements in air travel, that advantage is much more minimal. Though there are other ways they could use such a portal for nefarious purposes. We find ways to deal with those that misuse it. Travelers find ways to get the people to rise up against such people."

"Was William Clark a Traveler?"

"No, but he had the aid of one. He was a man of morals and action. Who better to be utilized to take down a tyrant and lift up the people? He had a guide that helped him find the portal. Toby had long been teaching the native tribes more advanced farming and hunting techniques, so when the opportunity came to relieve the Hasabi of their King, Toby made sure that the portal was open and ready for Clark to 'discover'."

"So, what is it that we are supposed to do, as Travelers?"

"The short answer is to live your life, spreading love, peace, and serenity to those in your sphere. It is immensely contagious. But you will also fight for freedom and defend the downtrodden in your journeys. Ignoring the plight of people in bad situations will never be the answer. The long answer will have to wait, until you have been educated on the history of the Traveler."

"Haven't we been working on that?"

"The history of the world is far longer than you know, the history of the Travelers is just as long. We have breached only on a couple that I knew would get your attention. To understand the role, you must first understand the nature of man, and the evolution of that nature. Professor, I know that you have been immersed in other cultures, though mostly middle-eastern, in your career. Do you typically see the similarities, or the differences?"

Stuart thought about that for a moment before responding, "Obviously there are differences, but in order to do the work that I do, you have to look for similarities. You have to find some basis to bond and build trust and a relationship on."

"Okay, and James in the meeting rooms of Alcoholics Anonymous, do you see similarities, or do you see differences?"

James' eyes opened in surprise. *How does he know all of this stuff about our lives? It's not like he has a computer or even a file that he's reading from.*

"So much for anonymity. But I suppose when you first come into the rooms you are focused on differences, mostly because nobody wants to admit that they belong there. But as you grow through the program, you see everyone as very similar. Of course, that group has a lot of shared experiences that they can relate with. Stuff that would make normies cringe."

"Normies?" asked Adon.

"Non-alcoholics...normies, or normal people. Whatever that means."

"Indeed, whatever that means. Here's the thing: All humans have more shared experiences than differences, birth, hunger, love, wealth, poverty, death of loved ones, the struggle to provide for their kids.

The list is long, yet too many focus on the differences. This causes division, strife, racism, classism, genocide, anger and war. It is horrific what humankind is capable of doing to each other over some perceived difference. But every time there is a disaster, on a large scale, those differences fall away and love and compassion prevail and bring people together. This sad fact, that it takes catastrophe to bind people together is both what breaks my heart, and what gives me hope. Hope that mankind can learn to be that way in good times, too. Last time, that hope almost died in me."

"Last time?"

Adon paused, as if he was unsure whether to this open and honest this early in the process. *Alas, the truth is always the way.*

"This is the third cycle of humanity. The species has failed twice before, destroying itself in the process. Despite our efforts, this cycle seems to be evolving in the same direction."

"You keep saying 'our' and 'we', yet you keep telling us that the gods were misunderstood, or consciously elevated to that status. So, who besides you are you talking about?" Stuart asked.

"The duality of existence. We are all individuals and, yet, we are all one. We are unique... just like everyone else. We are all in this together, yet individual responsibility plays a huge role in how things evolve. The irony is that we are nothing but energy, the same energy. But the way that energy is expressed creates a kaleidoscope of differences."

"What do you mean third cycle? Like, before the flood and after? What was the other one?" James asked.

"No, the great flood was in this cycle. A do-over, if you will, after the evolution was tainted. Mankind needed a reboot. They never recovered from the influences of Satah, a Traveler that I misjudged completely. The flood was my fault. That is why I tried to save some from each culture, so we didn't have to start from the beginning again. Though we started nearly fresh, Satah's influence was never erased completely and over time it festered and grew again."

"Wait, you've been here for five thousand years?"

'Me? Oh no..." he smiled a distant smile, full of both joy and pain, "it has been far, far longer than that. But time is a funny thing. It speeds up and slows down, it goes forwards and back, minutes can grow long, but years fly by. Here in the Garden of Adin, time stands still, and yet all times are happening at once. Everything that has ever happened, or ever will happen is happening simultaneously. I know it is difficult to understand, but the only 'now' that exists is found at the crossroads between the different planes of existence."

"If everything happens simultaneously, then how

can we change things?"

"Everything is interconnected. If we impact someone, positively or negatively, they will then spread the effect of that to those that they come into contact with. If you walk up to a stranger and punch them in the nose, their anger and resentment over that act will be carried with them all day causing them to take their frustration out on others. Conversely, a simple act of kindness can lift someone's spirit, and that is what they spread and share with the world."

"Sounds like a virus."

"Indeed, it spreads like a virus too. This is why in English you say 'spread joy' or 'spread holiday cheer' instead of something like 'create joy'. You can create it for yourself, but you can only spread it to others. Part of the reason that I wanted you to deal with your dark clouds was so you could let go and have inner peace, for you cannot transmit something that you do not possess."

"I have to ask... If you are such a peaceful guy, why do you have the flaming sword?" James queried.

"Because, as I said, all life begins here in the garden, as does all knowledge. Therefore, it must be protected. There are many who would destroy this place if given a chance, especially since the time of Satah. I am its father, its attendant, its nurturer, its caregiver, and yes, its protector."

"In the bible, Uriel is said to have been given a sword of flame to watch over the Garden of Eden after Adam and Eve were cast out. Does that make you Uriel? Are you an Archangel?"

Adon considered this question for a moment, "The real answer is both yes, and no. Though the explanation of that answer will have to wait until further into your training. You wouldn't be able to grasp it at this point."

"What kind of training?"

But I will say that, though your mission will be to spread love, peace, serenity, and freedom, it is not all hugs and roses. There will be times where you will have to fight for those things. Too many times, I am afraid. People in power tend to dislike either peace or freedom, at least for the people that they rule. Empowering the people diminishes the power of the ruling class, they rarely relinquish that power willingly. In the past we have tried mass empowerment, via religious movements, but ultimately, the same egos that craved the control of their kingdoms and empires gained control of the religious movements and changed them into something else entirely different than what they were intended to be. Absolution via worship in a building, with forgiveness granted by priests with their own rules caused people to stop seeking truth and connecting with the spirit of the universe. Instead they became comfortable and content with sitting and listening to someone preach his interpretation of the way things were. If they only knew how wrong they were about everything." He paused and shook his head. "Don't get me wrong, some of the priests, pastors, and imams have done a great job of spreading love, peace and freedom to their flock, but they were doing it from within a totally flawed system. If they were individuals, instead of representatives of an institution it would have been fabulous. Never forget that it is the connection of the individual to the universe that is the way, the answer, not the connection to any book or figure. All of the answers lie within you, and everyone else. You have forgotten how to make that connection. That will be mankind's downfall."

Stuart changed the subject, "There was a large stone outside the gate, or portal, that we found. It had markings from dozens of languages, eras, and cultures. We have been calling it the Waypoint Stone, but do you know if there was any purpose for it? Or was it simply a guest book, of sorts? Also, how long have these gates existed? They seem both futuristic and ancient."

"Alas, though we discourage ego driven actions, humans—even the best of them—often can't resist the urge to leave their mark on the world. Of course, it is entirely possible that it was left specifically to get your attention."

"Some of these were languages that have been dead for thousands of years. How could it have been left for us?"

"What better way to attract the attention of an archaeologist than to leave dead languages in places that they shouldn't be? Remember, on this plane it is now, but on the other planes of existence now might be five thousand years ago. Everything is connected."

"But what was the purpose of the portal, then? Why build it in a remote area that had no civilization anywhere near it?"

"They were all remote areas when they were built. They were built at the end of the first cycle when we began using Travelers to save it from itself. We were too late. But there are now seven gateways, one on each continent. That way, travelers could get to any place in the world where they were needed."

"So, the myths were right, kind of, about the Seven Cities of Gold." James said.

"Kind of." Stuart replied, deep in thought. "Wait, all seven continents? Obviously, we're in Asia and we came from North America. But that means South America, Australia, Europe, and Africa makes six. Did you really build one on Antarctica? Why, there is nothing but a bunch of scientists there?"

"Perhaps that is true now, but that doesn't mean that it was always the case." Adon smiled. "But even if you are correct, yes there are a bunch of scientists there, but it is also the most hotly contested land-mass on earth. Governments from most of the in-dustrialized world have broken it up into sectors of autonomous rule. Claims, if you will. If things go badly, well, you could definitely foresee a need for a traveler to go there. Especially, if they ever figure out that they are studying the wrong things."

"The wrong things?"

"Never mind. You don't get all of the answers, yet. You must uncover most of them yourself. Training begins tomorrow. Go home, eat, and get some rest. Tomorrow you will need it. Come back up the gate at dawn tomorrow, and be ready for anything."

"Thank you Adon. We appreciate your guidance and knowledge."

"This too shall pass. You will curse me before this is all over, but then you will find true under-standing. Learning and growth, especially spiritual growth, requires you to learn to be comfortable in your discomfort. For it is discomfort that motivates us to finally change things. Good intentions offer the world nothing. Good actions, even under duress, are what changes the world."

CHAPTER THIRTY-THREE

Augustine and Angeline climbed the ramp, eager to learn more from Adon. Sleep seemed hard to come by as their minds were spinning, trying to make sense of all that Adon had told them, and all that he hadn't. In some ways it felt like a get-to-know-you conversation, though Adon seemed to know everything about them already. Answers came in vague anecdotes and segways into other areas. The only direct answer that pertained to their new roles was that they were to spread love, peace, and freedom in all aspects of their lives. In retrospect, the role sounded like the lyrics to a song from Woodstock. Briefly he had the image of Jesus and the Amazing Technicolor Dreamcoat pop into his head.

James looked over to Stuart as they neared the

top of the ramp, "I wonder what Adon has planned for our training."

"We're about to find out."

A flash of light and a slight breeze met them as they began to walk down the ramp. They walked down casually. James noticed it first. There was no lava pit powering this cavern. This wasn't the gate to Adon and the Garden, they were somewhere new.

High atop the inner peak of the pyramid the, wind blew through long vertical slits in the stone and caught the faces of an unusual wind-turbine made up of dozens of razor thin blades causing it to rotate rapidly. It was truly amazing how in every chamber they let the most prominent natural resource in the area power each gateway.

"Did you bring the satellite transponder?" He asked Stuart.

"No, I thought we were just going to Adin."

"Crap. The question I have is, did we choose the wrong symbol, or is this a test?"

"Well, let's go face whatever we have to face."

James adjusted the holster inside his waistband, not because it needed to be adjusted, but because insecurities about the unknowns that they were going to face made it necessary for him to reassure himself that all was well.

They stepped into the winding tunnel, floral and citrus aromatics wisped through the air. When they reached the final turn, James paused and took a deep breath and they stepped out the opening and onto the ledge. The view was full of stunning grass covered mountains and deep cleft valleys that all seemed to ring a single flat meadow.

The scene would have been serene had it not been for the dozens of men fighting each other with long swords and long spears. They all wore similar flowing robes with wide flaring pants of varying colors. Some wore intricately designed breastplates that appeared to be made of thick leather. They fought aggressively, hacking, twirling, and jabbing ferociously, but with an elegance and grace in their movements that James and Stuart had only ever seen in old Samurai movies.

"What have we walked into? Some sort of tribal squabble?" Stuart asked.

"I don't know, but it's fascinating. Look how fluidly they move."

Motion in James' periphery caused him to move just a fraction of an inch to see what it was. An arrow clanged off the rock next to his ear, right where his face would have been had his instincts not made him turn.

"Get down!" James shouted as he pulled Stuart to the ground. He glanced around looking for cover. Because of their high-ground position, being on the ground protected them, but that would only last until the warriors reached them. No, they had to move now, before they were trapped.

The entrance to the cavern was only about ten yards from where they were. "Maybe we should just head back to the gateway." James suggested.

"But what if this is a test? What if Adon planned this to see whether we would cut and run? There has to be another way."

"Either way, let's get into the cave and get some cover while we figure out what's next. Come on."

James sprang to his feet and ran toward the opening salvo of arrows rained down in front of the opening. James dove to his left and rolled up against the face of the mountain. "Okay, that didn't work."

Stuart crawled over to where James was, as another volley of arrows blocked the cave opening. "Let's go down. I don't like it, but I like sitting here like a wounded duck even less."

James pulled pistol out of his waistband and nodded. He started to move down the path, when Stuart reached out and grabbed his arm. "Remember, love, peace, and freedom. That's why we are here. Put that away for now."

"So, what do you want to do? Waltz down there with our hands up and hope they don't kill us on the spot?"

"I think we walk down there confidently, not submissively. But also, not aggressively. We defend ourselves, but we don't go on offense. We'll see how they respond when they see we are unafraid, but have no intent to hurt them."

"Sure, the thirty or forty guys down there with swords and spears, plus who knows how many with bows, I am sure they are worried about whether we 'intend' to hurt them." He said sarcastically. Still, he put the handgun into its holster and nodded his consent.

They walked down the path, staying close to the wall so as not to give the archers an angle. As the path wound around the final turn it terminated at the entrance to the small open meadow. James said a short prayer for strength and they marched on.

Most of the warriors continued fighting each other as if they had no inkling that the archers had attacked Angeline and Augustine, or that intruders were inbound to the battle. The nearest warrior to them lay in a heap on the ground, blood spraying in the air.

James ran over to the man and knelt down beside him. Blood sprayed from a gash on his thigh. James was no doctor, but he had seen enough war movies to know that it was probably the femoral artery that had been cut. If he didn't do something the man might only have seconds to live. He jammed his hand onto the wound, and tried to put pressure on the wound. Blood squirted between his fingers and he readjusted his hands, putting pressure on a slightly different spot. The bleeding didn't stop, but it did stop spraying. That must be better.

"Stuart, give me your belt." He called out.

"My belt?"

"We need to make a tourniquet, to stop the bleeding, and I am not wearing a belt. Come on, now!"

Stuart pulled the belt from his waist, knelt down alongside James, and wrapped it around the man's upper thigh, pulling it tight before tying it off.

Neither man noticed how quiet the tribal skirmish had become, they were too busy trying to save the man on the ground. James slowly released the pressure to be sure that the bleeding had been staunched. As he pulled away, he looked up to celebrate with Stuart and noticed that all of the warriors from both sides of the battle now surrounded them, looking none too friendly. Stuart and James both stood. The temptation to raise their hands in submission was strong, but they both refrained.

Instead, Stuart put his out palms up to try to calm the situation, "Hi, we mean you no harm. We come in peace." The words tumbled out, without a thought, in perfectly fluent Japanese.

James looked at him with his mouth half open. The warriors disappeared from his thought and all he could focus on was the fact that his friend just spoke Japanese.

The crowd parted and a short lean warrior glided into the circle, face covered with a balaclava and an elaborately stitched breastplate of crimson leather. Clearly, this was the leader of one of the clans. He paced back and forth quickly and gracefully. Finally, he turned, swung his sword at full speed toward James neck, stopping with the snap of a wrist mere millimeters from the skin.

"Why are you here?" He asked, in softer tone than was expected.

James was baffled, not by the question itself, but by the fact that he understood it as clearly as if he was Japanese himself.

"I think that maybe we were sent, specifically to help him," he replied in perfect Japanese, pointing to the warrior on the ground. "What is this place, anyway?"

"Are you armed?"

James nodded and lifted his shirt so they could see the concealed handgun in his hip holster.

"Interesting. So, despite, arguably, being better armed, you chose compassion over either fear or violence."

The warrior pulled the sword away from his neck and turned away from them, then pulled off the mask. "This is the training ground." When he turned around, it became clear that he wasn't a he at all. She was strikingly beautiful, but clearly menacingly deadly. Her nearly-violet colored eyes looked right through him. "I am Ava. We," she gestured to her men, "will be your trainers."

"I thought we were spreading love, peace, and freedom. Why are we training to be warriors?"

"So that you can live long enough to spread love, peace, and freedom. The world is an ugly place at times."

James and Stuart looked at each other and shrugged, "Let's do it."

EPILOGUE

October 11, 1809

He took a final drag from the bottle that he had
been drinking since early morning. Life hadn't
worked out the way he had planned, and he simply
couldn't go on. He had been named Governor of the
Louisiana Territories, and been given a land grant
for leading the great expedition west. But battles
with his secretary, Mr. Bates, over funding and a few
bad business deals had stretched his finances to the
limit. The U.S. War office had also failed to reimburse him for many of his expenses from the expedition, primarily based on testimony from Bates. This
forced Lewis to sell off his newly acquired land and

give up his office. The depressing turn of events also contributed to his extremely close relationship with whisky. That didn't help his situation.

His plan had been to travel to Washington D.C., via a ship out of New Orleans, and work out his reimbursement issues in person. On the way there, he had another idea. He knew what had plagued him all of these years. He called on Will to help him. He didn't want to live this life anymore, not in this ungrateful country, anyway.

The two rode mostly in silence down the familiar path. They got off their horses near the levy that they had built. They stood on the dry-side, in the riverbed and scrutinized the way the rocks had fallen.

"We shouldn't need more than a trickle to get it going again, and you need to be able to plug it up when I am gone."

Will hated to see the great man that he had once known had become a penniless, bitter old drunk. But he owed the man. It was a debt that he needed to repay. If this was the way, then so be it.

"If we take that one out," he said pointing to a second level stone, "I should be able to pry that one up and over to fill the gap. Are you sure that you want to do this?"

Lewis burped before responding, "There is nothing left for me here. Maybe I will find something worth living for there. And if not, I am no worse off there than here."

"Why don't you walk in before I open the flood-gates? I am not certain that you would survive swimming in after all these years."

"Okay, if you think you can handle it on your own. Thank you, my friend. I know that you don't want me to do this, but the fact that you are here anyway means a great deal to me. You're the only one that didn't turn on me. Goodbye, my friend."

"Goodbye, I hope you find whatever you are looking for. What should I tell everyone?"

"Tell them that I am dead. I don't want any sympathy now. Hell, tell them that I killed myself. Tell them whatever you want to." With a tip of his hat Meriwether turned away.

Will watched his friend walk into the tunnel. After a few minutes, he dug the steel rod in behind the stone that they had decide upon and gave it a push. He watched the water flow down the riverbed.

"Goodbye, old friend."

THE END

TRUTH VS. FICTION

Though there is a plethora of notes and journals that Lewis & Clark and others in their party wrote, there are indeed some missing, unaccounted for journal entries. This fact, led me to pick three particular days while they were in Idaho with Chief Cameahwait's tribe and hypothesize about what they might have done during those days... of course, my imagination ran wild.

Meriwether Lewis was indeed a secretary to President Jefferson and the stories about how the expedition came to be, and William Clark's recruitment, are largely factual, except of course, for the secret side mission to find Cibola.

I went back and forth about whether to include the Epilogue. I wanted to bring the story back around to Will & Meri. But another action sequence seemed ill fitting. The truth is Meriwether was made Governor amongst other things, but whispers of corruption and interpersonal problems exacerbated by the government's refusal to reimburse his expenses caused financial despair on top of everything else. He reportedly drank too much and became a depressed bitter man. Reports vary about exactly how he died. He was indeed headed to Washington DC to face the War department and try to get paid, but like in the story he deviated from his initial plan, and went a different way. Within days he was dead, some say he was murdered; others say it was suicide. Either way, I prefer to think he found peace in some exotic land.

While wildfires are quite common, the references to the #BonnFire which destroyed James' hometown of Genna came from my first novel, BURN SCAR, which was a fictional take on a very real disaster... The #CampFire which destroyed the town of Paradise, California on November 8th, 2018. Genna is the Maltese word for Paradise. But that was James Augustine's origin story. I liked the character, and his flaws, so much that I wanted to keep him going forward as I went back to writing a more traditional Historical Thriller. So, I paired him up with an archaeologist, Stuart Angeline. The professor's origin story, SAND SCAR, will be released in the next couple of months and Book #2 of the Augustine & Angeline series, TIME SCAR, will follow in the first half of 2020.

The Garden of Adin, was an unexpected twist that even I didn't see coming. As for the stories of gods and men from the past, who knows what is true and what isn't, so I tried to give them all a common link... they were Travelers, trying to spread love, peace, and freedom.

Runes in America: there is plenty of evidence that Vikings came to America long before Christopher Columbus. The Newport Tower and the Kensington Runestone are the most well-known, but a number of other finds, mostly along the northern portion of the U.S. and along the St Lawrence River. It would be an interesting topic to explore at some point in the future.

If you would like some hints about what is coming next for Angeline & Augustine, follow me and sign up for my newsletter at https://wordsmithmojo.com/newsletter/